The Fountain

* *

The Fountain

* *

Betsy Johnson-Miller

North Star Press of St. Cloud, Inc.
St. Cloud, Minnesota

Once again it was a pleasure to have Mary Bruno do the art for the cover—her work makes the book come alive.

ISBN-13: 978-0-87839-409-8

First Edition, May 1, 2011

Printed in the United States of America

Published by
North Star Press of St. Cloud, Inc.
P.O. Box 451
St. Cloud, Minnesota 56302

www.northstarpress.com

—for my mother

1

But how?" Dokken Carver asked over his shoulder as Litney Way followed him through the weeds. Litney had just finished telling him about everything that had happened with the bracelet—from the magic backpacks they had both received to how she'd been able to fly. The two of them were headed out into the wetlands that took up acres and acres of land behind Dokken's new house. His parents had moved to Minnesota almost two months ago, coming from New York City. They had moved from the land of skyscrapers and flashing billboards to a town without even one stoplight. It wasn't that Dokken didn't like Minnesota. He just couldn't get over the land—how it went on and was everywhere. Dokken took a moment to absorb everything Litney had told him about this adventure they were supposed to have had, and then he said, "No way. It isn't possible."

"That's what I thought," Litney replied with an understanding nod. "Think about it, though. One morning I decide to go to a garage sale when that's something I've never done before. There I find a bracelet, and when I get home, I discover a note from my own mother in the lining of the box. I mean, I hadn't even shown the box or bracelet to my mother yet, so she didn't have any time to put the note in there herself. She didn't even know I had it. And then when I did talk to her about it, she told me this wild story about how she had had the bracelet and so had my grandmother. That night we headed to my grandparents' farm and I went out to the Atrium. You came in right after I heard the birds talking, and . . . ." Here Litney grinned. "Then off we went."

"Uh huh."

She giggled. "You were in totally rumpled clothes, wearing only one sock." She looked at the red-headed Dokken ahead of her as they trekked through the weeds and laughed some more. "Kind of like now. Those . . . those are the very same pants and shirt, I think."

"Ha ha." He cut her a scowl over his shoulder, even though he knew she was probably right—he wore these clothes all the time. "But I died," Dokken came back to this detail for the third time, looking at Litney with his blue eyes. That fact kind of blew the rest out of the water.

"Yes," Litney said.

"But I'm not dead," he insisted. It was a pretty important point. He turned forward again and kept walking. "And I don't remember dying. You'd think if *you* died, you'd remember it," he muttered. He liked Litney. He really did. Even though he'd only known her a couple of months, she was already the best friend he'd ever had. Maybe the only real friend he'd really ever had. But she was crazy. Certifiably nuts. How in the world could he have magically appeared in Minnesota even though he'd been asleep in his bed in New York? How could he have gone to a different world, different dimension, or whatever, where animals talked? How could he have read Litney's mind and how could she, an ordinary girl, fly?

And this bracelet. It magically appears; it magically disappears. That didn't make any sense at all. But even if all that was true, and he was sure it wasn't, there was no way he could have died. That kept hitting him like the big old meat mallet his mother used to tenderize chicken. On the other hand, somehow, miraculously, his parents had up and decided to move to Minnesota, with no discussion he heard, and he had ended up in the same school as Litney . . . and this had happened after he had died, even though he was now . . . not . . . dead.

It was crazy, and thinking about this whole thing gave him the willies. He glanced back again at Litney, wishing he'd stayed home and slept in this morning instead of coming out here with her. That way, this conversation never could have happened, and he wouldn't have to be wondering if he was going to stay friends with her or not.

"That's why I was so thrilled to see *you* when I stepped into the principal's office two months ago, because it meant you weren't really dead,"

Litney explained as if that solved the whole thing. She undid the rubber band holding her curly brown hair and put it up again. Even though it was mid-October, it was still warm, and she wanted all that hair off her neck.

"I thought you were crazy when you screamed my name," he admitted, thinking now that his first impression of her might have been the correct one. Nuts.

"And what do you think of me now that I've told you all this?" She tried to keep her voice light, teasing, but she didn't quite succeed. When he didn't answer right away, she rushed on, "I know, I shouldn't have told you all this at once. I should have waited. Or never said anything. Ever." Litney couldn't say why she had chosen today to tell him about their adventure. The two of them had gotten to know each other pretty well the past couple of months. In fact, they had spent almost every weekend together since school began, but when she had thought time and again about telling him all of this, she had decided she would never tell him about their adventure together. She was too glad to have him as a friend. She didn't want to risk losing that. But for some reason, as they walked across these wetlands today in the early fall morning, she had felt her mouth open and the story come pouring out, almost like pop squirting out of a bottle that had been shaken up. There was no stopping it, no holding it back. "Look," Litney said quietly, "I don't blame you if you don't believe me. And I sure don't blame you if you don't want to, you know, be my friend anymore."

"No . . ." he said. He wanted to make her feel better by adding, "I'm glad you told me," but he couldn't. He would have been lying if he said that, so he clarified, "But you don't have the bracelet anymore?"

"Nope. Once I got back, I had to write a note to *my* future daughter, and then I had to put it back in the box." Litney's dark-brown eyes grew troubled. "Besides thinking you were dead, giving up the bracelet was one of the hardest things I've ever done."

"Do you think you'll ever get it again? Like when you turn sixteen? That's when you said your mother and grandmother received it, right?"

"Yes, but somehow I doubt it. I think I've had my chance."

Because of how she said that, he asked, "Do you even want it back?" He slapped at his neck then scratched the spot to get rid of the carcass of whatever insect had just bitten him.

"I don't know," she replied honestly. "It was scary when I had it. I really didn't know if I could survive any of it. Or make any difference." She closed her eyes and, even though the sun was warm on her face, she shivered. She remembered the dogs that had attacked them, the way Mala had pulled her under the water, the quiet and fear as she had waited for Mala's forces to attack. But then she remembered the delight of flying and the Song of Silence and the crushing loving hug of Asta the bear. She repeated, "I don't know."

They had reached the papery-white birch trees whose leaves were just beginning to yellow. This was further than they had ever ventured into the wetlands before, but they had packed a lunch, so they could be out in the fields and trees all day. "What's that?" Litney asked, pointing through the trees to a space ahead of them.

"Can't tell," Dokken answered, squinting. "Some sort of old building, maybe."

"And, look, there are more buildings over there. Do you see that one? I'll bet this is an old abandoned farm. Wanna explore?" Litney asked.

Dokken kind of wanted to go home. He needed some time to think about what Litney had told him. No, that wasn't true. He needed time to think about Litney. She didn't look crazy as she stood there waiting for him to answer, but what about all those things she had told him? She was bananas. She had to be.

But he didn't really want to walk back through the wetlands alone—he wasn't sure what he'd meet, he wasn't sure if he knew the way—so he shrugged and said, "Yeah, I guess. Whatever."

"YOU'D BETTER HAVE A DARN GOOD REASON to be nosing around my property," a deep voice roared behind them. They jumped and turned. Standing behind them was probably the tallest man either of them had ever seen. He had brown bushy hair like his head was covered in grizzly bear fur, and right next to his Adam's apple, Litney noticed a birthmark that looked like a surprisingly accurate rendition of the state of Florida.

Dokken and Litney slowly backed away from the barn they had been peering into. Without realizing what they were doing, the two of them had inched closer and closer together until they bumped into one another. Litney decided this was ridiculous. He was just a man after all. She straightened herself up and threw her shoulders back. "You live here?" she asked. She hadn't meant for it to come out like that, like a demand. Really she had been asking in disbelief. The house to their left was made out of stones bigger than her head, and it seemed solid enough. The roof, though, looked so rotten that it seemed as if it would collapse if the tiniest bird landed on it. Not only that, but the roof had an entire corner missing. Litney guessed at least a quarter of the house was without protection from the weather. What did he do in the rain? In winter?

"What's it to you if I live here? Why don't you get on home." It was not a request.

"Who's there?" a woman's voice asked from inside the house. "Talmoon Strange, do we have visitors?"

"Never you mind, dear," the man's voice answered, and though it was still deep, now there was a suggestion of softness to it that hadn't been there before.

"Are you being your lovely welcoming self?" a woman asked as she stepped out the door. Her hair, long and tightly curled, was mostly shiny black, but it had tiny strands of silver woven throughout it. Her face, a soft brown color, was lightly lined. Somehow she managed to look old and young at the same time. Perhaps that was because her face glowed, like an ancient moon. Her eyes were her most startling feature. It wasn't just that they were so large they seemed to take up half her face; it was their color. Litney had brown eyes herself, but her eyes were of the darkest brown, so that they almost bordered on black. This woman's eyes were brown but also golden, like holding syrup up to the sun.

Dokken, on the other hand, decided the woman looked like a willow tree—long and flowing. He was pretty sure this woman had to have been a dancer at some point in her life.

"Pansy, you get on back in the house. These two young'uns were just leaving."

"Now, Talmoon, why would I want to do that when I could share some of my fresh sugar cookies and lemonade with them? Sound good?" she asked Litney and Dokken as she crossed the yard to reach up on her tippy toes and kiss her husband's shoulder. She had to kiss his shoulder because there was no way she was going to reach his cheek since he wasn't bending down to accommodate her.

"We don't want to be a bother," Litney said as she took a step backward. "We didn't know anyone lived out here." As she looked around, she realized there was no road leading to the house. How did they leave to go to town and get groceries and such? Did they ever leave? Maybe they waited for children to wander into their yard, and then they ate them. Hansel and Grettel popped into her mind. No. The man scared the goosebumps out of her, but the woman, Pansy was it? She seemed kind.

"We won't bother you again," Dokken said, staring at the man who was a mix of terrifying similes—not only did Talmoon have a voice as big as thunder, but he also looked like a tree about to fall on Dokken, squashing the very life and breath out of him. Or with that hair he looked like a huge mean bear who could make Dokken's guts spill out all over the dirt with one swipe of his hand. Dokken wanted to get away from here, now.

The woman with the curly black hair and golden eyes laughed and then she leaned in to whisper to Dokken, "I felt the same way."

"What do you mean?" Dokken asked in his own whisper, his eyes never leaving the big man.

"About him." She jerked her thumb at her husband, who suddenly didn't seem quite so tall or threatening. "The first time I met him, all he did was turn to look at me and say, 'What do you want?'" Pansy mimicked his low rough voice and stood on her tippy toes again. Then she laughed her musical laugh. "I turned and ran just like you want to do right now."

Instead of letting the two teenagers escape, however, Pansy hooked her arms through theirs and walked them toward the house. "You see, I'd heard about this man who made the most beautiful teapots anyone had ever seen. It was because of my grandmother that I cared about teapots at all. She was from England, and she lived in the house next door to ours when I was growing up. Every afternoon at 3:30, I would go over there, wearing white gloves, mind you, and the two of us would have tea. Her teapot was made of fine bone china, and it was covered in roses so real-looking that when I left, I swore I had their lovely scent in my nose. So, after I had grown, when I heard there was a great potter in these wetlands, I decided I was going to meet him and ask him if I could be his apprentice so I could learn to make my own beautiful teapots. I never dreamt I'd end up being his wife."

By this time Pansy had led them into the house. She motioned for Litney and Dokken to sit at a long wooden table the color of honey while she turned to busy herself at a kitchen counter made of the same wood. Litney looked up to see if this was where the hole in the roof was, but no, above her were rafters and roof that seemed as solid and whole as her own at home.

The stove in the corner had a pile of wood beside it, and cast iron pots sat on top of it. A big metal rack screwed into the wall behind the stove held more pots and pans, and it didn't take long to realize there were collections of wooden spoons everywhere—in vases like flowers, in piles on the counter, even three in Pansy's back pocket.

"You must like spoons," Litney observed.

"Sure do. For the longest time, I was always looking for a spoon, to stir this or mix that. I had two, and they were always dirty or hiding. So for a while, every time I went to the store, I bought a pack. Now I never have to look for a spoon because they're everywhere. Plus, I like to keep things stirred up," the woman said devilishly as she sashayed around the kitchen, humming as she opened this and closed that.

"You know, it took me awhile to find this place when I was looking for Talmoon," Pansy told them, taking one of the spoons out of her back pocket to give a good stir to the pitcher of lemonade she had just pulled from the refrigerator. The refrigerator, about a third of the size of a normal fridge, looked like something the seven dwarves might have used, and inside Litney was sure she had seen a big block of ice sitting on one of the shelves.

"It would be hard to find," Litney agreed. "I noticed there was no road."

"An observant girl you are. Nope, there's no road. Talmoon Strange has never liked visitors." The wild-haired woman turned to look at them, her face amused. "I know, a real surprise. But I just had to find him. I was at this small teashop one day, and when the waitress brought out my tea and toast, she put a pot on the table that was so incredible it reached right into my lungs and pulled out every bit of air in there."

"What did it look like?" Dokken asked, who had relaxed some. Pansy had set a plate of melt-in-your-mouth sugar cookies in front of them. Dokken had already finished his first and reached for a second.

"Have you ever noticed how the most beautiful or unique things are hardest to describe?" Pansy asked, her eyes aglow as she slid next to him on the bench. "Like a rose. How can you find the words to do it justice? Or all those stars up there on a clear night. Stars and roses and Talmoon's teapots are bigger than words."

"That must have been one amazing teapot," Litney said, and maybe it was, but, honestly, how could a teapot be that awesome? Pansy just loved her husband—that's why she was so ga-ga over his work.

"You don't believe me," Pansy said to Litney, and while she was smiling, the woman had one shiny black eyebrow arched in what looked like a challenge.

"Oh, no, I do. I'm sorry. I do," Litney stammered.

"No, you don't, but that's okay. I'll tell you what," Pansy said. "Remember that barn the two of you were looking in when Talmoon found you?"

Both Litney and Dokken nodded. They wouldn't be forgetting that for a very long time. Truth be told, neither of them would be surprised if that moment were to make its way into a nightmare soon.

"Why don't you go back out there and dig around a little?" Pansy suggested.

"Oh, no," Dokken said. "That's okay. Litney believes you, don't you, Litney?" He glared at her because he did not want to go back out there where that big man was, and he definitely did not want to start poking around his property. No thank you. He didn't care if they were going to be looking for gold, let alone a stupid teapot—he wasn't going.

"I'm serious," Pansy said. "Go out to that barn and poke around."

"Why?" Litney asked.

"Because he keeps his rejects out there. The pots he doesn't think are good enough."

Litney didn't ask it aloud, but Pansy could tell what the girl was thinking. "Why would you look at his rejects to see how beautiful his work is? Trust me."

"DID WE DO ANYTHING THIS STUPID on our first adventure together?" Dokken whispered as they neared the barn. They were coming at it sideways, moseying even, so as not to raise anyone's—Talmoon's—alarm.

"Stupid? No. Not really."

"So why are we doing it now?" he demanded.

"I don't kn—" They were just about to the barn when a crazy black-and-white thing darted at them. It rammed Litney in the leg, causing her to bump into Dokken. "Ouch!" she cried, but even before the word was out of her mouth, the creature had done the same thing to Dokken, and he had bumped back into Litney.

"Is that a dog?" Dokken asked, the two of them huddled together like sheep.

"I think so, but what's it doing?" Litney wondered.

"Herding you." It was that big voice again. "Current, here." The dog obeyed the command and immediately sat at Talmoon's left foot, leaning into his master's leg. He had to have eyes somewhere, but it was hard to see them, because two black patches of fur had landed on his face right where his eyes should have been. The dog's face was turned upward, fervently waiting to see what his master wanted him to do next.

It was that absolute concentration that helped Litney remember where she'd seen dogs like this before—in a documentary about New Zealand. Her parents were always making her watch documentaries, "because that's the only kind of TV that makes you smarter," they said. She remembered those dogs were so intense when it came to herding sheep that they had almost seemed insane. Litney had watched as the dogs had sat trembling, waiting for their masters to give them the sign that they could go herd, so eager for it they quivered. When they had finally been set free, the dogs had dashed all over the field until the sheep had flowed together and then poured like furry milk into the pen or pasture. What were they called, though? Border something. Border terriers? No . . . border collies. That was it.

"Your dog's name is Current?" Dokken asked, curiosity, for the moment, outweighing fear.

"Yep."

"I've never heard a dog called that before. Can I ask why?"

Talmoon didn't answer Dokken's question. Instead he posed one of his own. "Don't *ya* think it's time for *you* to be heading home?"

✷ 2 ✷

AFTER THE TWO OF THEM HAD hustled away from the farmstead—with Talmoon watching until he was sure they were good and gone—Litney didn't have any real time to talk to Dokken that next week. In school, the two of them had different class schedules, different lunch periods and lockers on different floors. After school, Litney had cross-country practice and then a load of homework to finish since she was taking two math classes, Spanish, and chemistry. This meant there wasn't any time to see Dokken after dinner either. Oh, he would smile and say, "Hi," when he passed her in the halls, but he never stopped even for a second to add, "How are you?" Nor did he call, and it was that fact that told Litney he no longer wanted to be her friend.

She was devastated . . . she wanted to go over to his house on Saturday and see if they could work it out somehow, but she couldn't. After a cross-country meet Friday evening, she had to go up to her grandparents' farm for the weekend and help them pick apples and make cider. Since her grandparents sold their cider to grocery stores around the state, this was a huge undertaking. Luckily, their farm was famous enough that there was always a horde of people eager to lend a hand. Not only were the bunkhouses overflowing with guests who wanted to be a part of this, but campers and tents had popped up all over the farm as well.

While Litney never liked doing chores around the house, she didn't mind working at her grandparents' farm. In August, she always looked forward to losing the lower half of her body (and sometimes the upper as well) amidst the vegetable plants she was harvesting. She loved the feel of the basket over her arm growing heavy with the bounty and the sight of the tables laden with reds and greens and purples, with orbs and ears and stalks.

And now in October, she loved climbing the ladders, getting her head lost in the branches and filling baskets with mounds of apples.

Plus, all this work was worth it because she had tasted the food her grandparents had grown. No other produce could compare. A strawberry from their farm put every store-bought strawberry she had ever eaten to shame. Litney loved wandering among the rows of the strawberry plants and plucking the best rubies of red flavor to pop in her mouth and savor.

But apple picking was her favorite. After the day of satisfying work was done, she couldn't wait to go to the pump behind the farmhouse, draw up some ice-cold well water and use her grandmother's special peppermint soap to clean up. She would lather her hands with the soap and then plunge them into the wooden bucket. The combination of the cold water on her skin and the peppermint in the soap made everything buzz, like a hundred bees were flying around in the veins of her hands.

Then, after she was done cleaning up, she got her chance to wander. Both laughter and smoke wafted around the campfires that dotted the farm's lawns, and normally she loved drifting from fire to fire and feasting and talking with everyone almost as much as she loved the picking of the apples. While her grandmother had told her getting to know the guests was "good business," Litney probably would have done it without being told. She thought it was great that people wanted to come to her grandparents' farm, and it was great to hear they had driven all the way from Kentucky or New Mexico. It was wonderful to compare farmer tans. And she was always glad to accept a piece of this or a taste of that as the groups made pies and muffins and roasted apples from the bounty. Plus, she almost always got a mug of hot chocolate or a chunk of brownie from them while she sat on a log a while and petted whatever kind of dog was there—big and goofy or small and feisty.

But tonight she sat alone on the porch swing, because she couldn't bring herself to be friendly. She was too worried. She was anxious to be done and return home. She didn't know what Dokken was thinking about her. Ever since she had told him about the bracelet and their adventure together, she had been sure he was done being her friend. She'd seen it in his eyes.

Litney thought about getting up and going inside, but she couldn't seem to get herself to move. She continued to swing, continued to listen to the sounds from around the yard, and pretty soon, Bernard, her grandparents' St. Bernard, wandered up the stairs from the yard and fell asleep under her swing. Not long after that, her grandfather found her as well. "Hey there, Litney Girl. What's going on?" he asked her as he sat down beside her on the swing and patted her knee. Bernard lifted his head only slightly before lowering it and falling once again into a snuffling slumber. Her grandfather chuckled at the sheer laziness of the dog, then said, "Ever since you got here, something hasn't felt quite right with you."

With anyone else she would have lied and said she was fine. But not with Pop, who was one of the few adults who talked with her, not to her. "I told Dokken about the bracelet."

He didn't answer for a moment, and Litney thought he maybe hadn't heard what she'd said. Gram was always saying he needed to get his hearing checked.

"Did you hear me?" she ventured.

"Course I did. Your grandmother doesn't know what she's talking about," her grandfather muttered. "My ears are fine. Just fine. I was just thinking before I spoke, something my grandfather taught me when I was your age. Something your grandmother would do right to remember. So, now, how did he take it?"

Litney quit examining the end of a piece of her hair and tucked it behind her ear. "I don't know. Not well. He looked at me like I was crazy."

"I'd like to remind you that you did the same thing to your mother," her grandfather said gently.

"What?"

"You looked at her like she was crazy. I remember sitting in there at the kitchen table the night you got the bracelet. You didn't believe a word your mother told you. Not until you went, that is."

"But I didn't know," Litney protested.

"Exactly," her grandfather said with a nod. "And Dokken doesn't remember. None of us do."

"What?" Litney exclaimed, and she stood up so quickly that she almost knocked her grandfather off the porch swing. Bernard's claws scrambled on the wood of the porch as he startled and tried to stand. When the dog realized there wasn't a serious threat in the immediate vicinity, he melted back down.

Her grandfather reached for her arm and pulled her back down beside him. He said, "It means there is always a boy who goes along."

While this was enough of a bombshell to have Litney's mouth hanging open in surprise, it was what occurred to her next that had her proclaiming, "Ohhh! Gross."

Even though Pop probably knew exactly what she was thinking, he played along and asked, "What? What's gross?"

"You mean I have to marry Dokken?" Litney sputtered.

"Why would *you* say that?"

"Because I'll bet *you* were the boy who went with Gram, and Dad was the boy who went with Mom. That's not fair. I should be able to choose who I marry. I don't want a . . . a . . . oh, what are those called. Those marriages where it's decided for *you*."

"Arranged marriage?" he offered.

"Yes. I don't want an arranged marriage!"

The more Litney spoke in exclamation points, the more softly her grandfather talked. "It's not an arranged marriage."

"But I'm right, aren't I? That *you* were the boy with Gram and Dad was the boy with Mom?"

"Yes."

"So how has it *not* been decided?" she demanded.

"Because *you* both get to decide. You get to choose."

"This is so weird." She was standing again, her hands balled into fists. "No wonder Dokken didn't believe me. Who would? Who would believe this? I can hardly believe it and I, at least, remember everything else."

"WHY'D SHE HAVE TO GO and tell me that?" Dokken asked himself aloud as he opened the door of his house and stepped out into the darkness. The garbage bag in his hand wasn't bulging full or dripping—as it often was—so Dokken wasn't in a rush to make it to the garbage can by the side of the garage. This gave him time to think, and when he had time to think, he usually ended up talking to himself. So tonight he went back to this question, the one he had been asking himself ever since their trek out into the wetlands last weekend. The bigger question, though, was what was he going to say to her when he saw her again? *Just how crazy are you?*

He hadn't intentionally avoided her this week, but he had to admit he was sort of glad he hadn't seen her all that much. And now it seemed like he was going to have even more time to ponder what he was going to say to her—his mom had just gotten off the phone with someone from the school. Apparently a water pipe had broken, and the school, which now had three feet of water in its lower level, was going to have to be shut down for the entire next week.

"Sweet," Dokken said aloud as he thought of the sleeping in this would allow him. This was followed by a completely unrelated thought: "At least it isn't one of those absolutely dark nights." Those kind of nights had taken him awhile to get used to. When he and his parents had first moved here, he had hated how dark it could get. Growing up in a city, Dokken was used to there always being a certain amount of light—streetlights or windows aglow no matter what time of the day or night it was. But here, there were no streetlights, and the nearest neighbor was a quarter of a mile away and hidden behind a hill. Only when the moon shone down like a flashlight was there any light out here. That meant much of the time there was this dark dark, and more often than not, when he was in bed, he couldn't even see his hand in front of his face.

Tonight, as he ambled down the three cement stairs to deposit the garbage in the can, he looked up and saw a quarter moon shining and gangs of stars taking advantage of the night. He couldn't really see, but he could at least make out vague shapes. Still, he walked slowly toward the direction of the garbage can because he had a feeling he might have forgotten to put away his skateboard.

"Dokken," a voice whispered, and the boy jumped.

"Wh-who's there?" he asked, and even though he might have been living in the middle of nowhere Minnesota, his New York City upbringing kicked in hard. He gripped the garbage bag tighter—it wasn't much of a weapon, but he would use it, if he had to. He could throw it all over the person and then run back into the house.

"It's me," whispered the voice, but for Dokken, there was no "me" to see.

"I'm armed." It wasn't a complete fabrication. Dokken knew there was a pile of nasty smelly yogurt inside the garbage bag that was sure to make any assailant puke. "I can hurt you, so you'd better just go."

"I can't," the voice responded.

Dokken had not intended to get into a conversation with his assailant, but the voice seemed to be coming at him from down low, so he couldn't stop himself from asking, "Where are you?"

"Down here."

Dokken looked down, and that's when he saw the crouched body. Even though he could now see a body that was talking to him, the creature stood far enough away from him that Dokken had to ask, " Who are you?"

"Current."

"What?"

"Current."

"Current? Like the dog Current?" Dokken asked, and that's when the dog rose and trotted closer. Dokken reached down with his hand, and sure enough, he felt fur. "But, but," the boy sputtered. "But you're talking!"

It appeared the dog could have cared less that this was surprising, because he didn't acknowledge that comment. Instead, he said simply, "I need your help."

"But you can *talk*," Dokken croaked, almost as if all the air had been knocked out of him.

"Yes, I can talk." The dog sounded bored.

"But animals can't talk." Wait. On his adventure with Litney, she had told him that animals could talk. Oh, man. Dokken worried that Litney had rubbed off on him and that he was now crazy. At the same time, he felt relief washing through him because maybe Litney wasn't a liar and maybe she wasn't crazy. On top of all this, there was a bit of joy that he was talking to an animal, something he had always dreamed of doing.

After the initial intensity of these emotions had stormed through him, it finally dawned on him what Current had said. "You need my help?"

"Yes. I need you to get your friend and come out to the farm." The dog turned and went back to where he had been standing. When Dokken didn't move, the dog urged, "You have to hurry."

"She's been gone the past couple of days. I don't know if she's home yet," Dokken said. "Should I wait till she gets back or do you want me to come with you now?"

The dog let out a sound that was nearly impossible to describe. It was like he was chewing a howl.

Dokken—who had never been around animals, not even fish—was sure that noise meant Current was about to bite him and drag him off into the wetlands as a late-night snack. The words, "Please don't hurt me!" rushed out of his mouth.

"That was *not* a growl," the dog said crisply, as if he might be offended. "I do that when I'm thinking. It clears my brain. For some reason, I thought you and your friend lived in the same place."

Dokken was sure he was blushing. Live with Litney? No way. "We live in the same town, not the same place. She lives about eight miles from here."

"Oh," the dog moaned. "If only there was a way you could talk to someone far away."

Dokken thought the dog was joking. "Um, the telephone?" he said, playing along.

"The what?"

"Telephone. You don't know what that is? Talmoon and Pansy don't talk on one?"

"Talmoon and Pansy don't have electricity. They don't even have an entire roof," the dog pointed out. "What does this telephone do?"

"I can pick it up and call Litney to see if she's at home."

"Like magic," Current nodded sagely.

"No. Not magic," Dokken argued. "It's technology."

"But you can't see her when you talk to her? And she can be very far away when you are talking to her?"

"Yes, of course. I can even talk on the phone to my uncle who is on a different continent."

"So, magic," the dog insisted.

The telephone, magic? "That's absurd," was what Dokken wanted to say to the dog, but then it struck him: for him a dog talking was magic, and he doubted Current would see it that way. Why wouldn't the dog see the phone as magic? "Interesting," Dokken said.

"What's interesting?" asked the dog.

"Nothing. Let me go inside and try calling her. I'll be right back. You wait here."

WITHIN THE HOUR, LITNEY'S MOTHER had pulled an old station wagon into Dokken's driveway. As Litney got out of the car, her mother rolled down the window and said, "Be careful."

"I will, Mom. And, hey, I don't know what's going on, or how long it'll take, but don't worry."

"I won't. I know you can handle it—plus, you have this entire week off from school, so take as long as you need."

Litney walked over to where Dokken was standing.

"You didn't have any trouble getting her to bring you over here, did you? Your mom was cool with this?" Dokken asked as he waved at the car backing out of the driveway.

"I told her a dog was talking to you."

"And she didn't find that odd?"

"Dokken, I told you," Litney said, more than a bit exasperated. "Animals talk when we have the bracelet."

"I know, it's just that . . . even though I was the one talking with him, I still find it odd."

"Do you believe me now?" Litney asked. She could barely see Dokken's face, only a glow over in his general direction from his pale skin.

"Yeah. Sorry I didn't before."

"That's okay. I'm not sure I would have if it had been me. I'm just glad this happened before I saw you again."

"Me, too," Dokken admitted. "I didn't know what I was going to say to you."

"It is odd, though," Litney said thoughtfully.

"I know. That's what I'm saying," Dokken said.

"No. What I mean is I'm not sure how this is happening. It's not like I have the bracelet or anything."

"Hello?" a third voice asked. "Is she here?"

"Hi, Current. Yes, I'm here," Litney said, bending down so she was eye to eye with the dog. Or at least she thought she was; she still couldn't see him very well. "Can you tell us what's going on?"

"Talmoon and Pansy were eating dinner when they came," the dog answered.

"When who came?" asked Dokken.

"These odd creatures. They must have snuck up on the farm. I didn't smell them. I should have smelled them." The dog spoke quickly and with obvious distress. "I mean I *usually* smell everything. I could smell you two from across the field and—"

"What did the creatures look like?" Litney asked.

"They had weird heads. Like a bird's. They were all these different colors . . . and furry like me, but they walked on their back legs," Current answered.

"Were they big?" Dokken wanted to know what they were up against. A tribe of Bigfoots that lived in the woods behind his house?

"Not as big as Talmoon, but yes, they were big," the dog replied. "Still, Talmoon would have fought them, I know he would have, if one of them hadn't shot a dart into his back. He fell out of his chair, and they carried him off. Miss Pansy put up a fight, though, until one managed to put a dart in her leg. Then she just hung over one's shoulder like a sack of dog food. I should have smelled them," Current repeated.

"Did you try and stop them?" Dokken asked.

"Of course I did," the dog snapped. Had it been lighter out, Litney and Dokken would have seen his lips curling so that his canines showed. "But I was asleep in my kennel when I heard the commotion. One of them must have locked the kennel before I woke up, because when I tried to help Pansy and Talmoon, I couldn't get out. I could only watch as they carried them away. I kept throwing my body at the fence, but it wouldn't budge. I just don't know why I didn't smell them. It's my job to protect them."

"How did you finally get out?" Litney asked, not caring a whit why Current's nose hadn't alerted him. "How did you get here?"

"I had to dig my way out under the fence, otherwise I would have been here sooner," the dog answered and began pacing back and forth.

"But why did you come here? Why not go to the police?" Dokken asked. He wished the dog had gone to the police.

"The police wouldn't be able to understand me," the dog replied.

"How did you know we would be able to understand you?" Litney asked.

"Miss Pansy said something after you left." The dog continued to move back and forth, and Litney guessed it was because he was upset. It was quite possible, though, he simply had that much energy. "She said the two of you had the magic about you. And Miss Pansy also said if something ever happened to her and Talmoon, then I should come here and get you."

"Do you think Pansy knew this was going to happen? She wasn't in on it, was she?" Dokken asked, and Current growled long and deep.

Dokken joked, "Are you clearing your brain so you can think again?"

"No. This time I was thinking about biting you," the dog replied bluntly. "Don't ever question Miss Pansy's intentions in front of me again."

Dokken backed away from the dog. "Okay, sorry. I was just asking."

"Why do you think Pansy said that, though?" Litney asked, not wanting to upset the dog, but still feeling this part of the story was important. "That you should come and get us if something happened. Had there been threats or other people around who made her uncomfortable?"

"Miss Pansy can sense things."

"You mean, she can see the future?" Litney clarified.

"Not necessarily see the future, but she can get this sense that something is going to happen. She'll say, 'I think it is going to rain soon,' even though the sky is pure blue, and then wouldn't you know it, about two hours later, it will rain. Or she'll say, 'Watch those trees over there. Something is gonna step outta there soon,' and before long, out will come two or three shy deer."

"Don't get mad at me," Dokken said to Current. "But I'm wondering why she couldn't sense these creatures were going to come."

"She must have. When they had coffee and cookies this afternoon, she said to Talmoon three times, 'I feel like something bad is about to happen.'"

"What did Talmoon say?" Litney asked.

"He didn't say anything, but he took her seriously enough to get his gun down from the mantle above the fireplace," Current replied. "That's when I went outside to my kennel. Talmoon and Pansy never lock me in, and so I thought I'd stay out there to keep watch rather than stretching out on the kitchen floor. But I couldn't see or smell anything, and I fell asleep."

Again, from the tone of his voice, it was easy to hear the dog's distress. He probably felt as if he had failed his master and Pansy.

"Why didn't Talmoon use the gun?" Dokken asked.

"Remember? He got a dart in the back," Litney answered Dokken, but then immediately shifted her attention back to Current. "What do you want us to do?"

"I need you to come with me," Current said, about to trot around the back of Dokken's house to head out into the wetlands.

"Wait!" Dokken exclaimed as Litney began to follow the dog. Even though he wouldn't have admitted it to anyone, he was both glad and disappointed all at the same time. "I can't go. My parents. I don't think they'll be as understanding as yours, Litney. It's not like I can go wandering around in the night without them noticing or wondering what in the heck I'm doing. Plus, I don't want to do that. My parents trust me, and I don't want to jeopardize that."

Current howled again in frustration.

"Okay, okay." Dokken said. "I'll . . . I'll go inside and ask them."

* 3 *

"I CAN'T BELIEVE THEY LET ME GO," Dokken said, shaking his head in the dark. His parents were nice and all, and he got along with them most of the time, but he never dreamed they would let him do this. He wasn't sure he was pleased.

"I guess that saying is true: the truth shall set you free," Litney replied with a smile in her voice.

After much talking (and howling by Current), the three of them had decided Dokken should tell his parents the truth—or at least as much truth as his parents could handle—and hope for the best. Dokken had told his mom and dad that some friends they had met out in the wetlands needed their help, and that he might be at their farm all night. Even as he had been saying the words, Dokken had been sure it wouldn't work. There was no way his parents were going to let him go out back in the dark for who knew how long. It was crazy to have even considered doing this, but apparently he hadn't taken Litney's innocent face into account. His parents liked her and trusted her, and, with surprisingly little discussion, they had decided Dokken and Litney would be fine. The only thing Dokken's mother had insisted on was that he take a cell phone with them. "You call us if you need us. Promise?"

"We promise. Hey, thanks, Mom." Without thinking, Dokken had hugged his mother and then looked at Litney to make sure she hadn't seen. She had, but she was kind enough to pretend she hadn't.

"I think it's great you want to go out and help some people," his father had said, pulling Dokken in for another embarrassing hug that was so big, it was impossible for anyone in the room to ignore.

Litney had stolen a glance at Dokken and his father as they had hugged. Even with their two red heads right next to each other, it had been difficult to tell whose hair was a more intense color. Probably Dokken's but only barely. The more she thought about it, the more she decided she liked Dokken's hair. Even though she had teased him about it when they first met, Litney realized his hair was vibrant and powerful. It demanded notice and was not about to stay shyly out of sight.

As the two of them had ended the hug, Dokken's dad had looked his son straight in the eyes and said, "Just be careful, son. Let us know if you need us."

"We will, Dad," Dokken said, the skin on his cheeks reddening. "Thanks."

Dokken's dad had then taken the opportunity to give his son one more hug. Only after Dokken had said, "Okay, Dad. Okay," did his dad let him leave.

Once they started walking away from the house, Litney and Dokken followed Current as quickly as they could. Even though they each had flashlights in their hands, compliments of Dokken's parents, they couldn't run nearly as fast as the dog wanted them to. There were simply too many weeds and roots and rabbit holes. Plus there was less moon now. Veils of clouds drifted over its face, darkening it and the night.

Litney and Dokken had forgotten how far away the farm was. "Are we getting close?" Dokken asked at one point as he wondered how fresh the batteries were in the flashlights. He did not want to be out here without any light.

"It's right over there," Current said, even though "over there" still looked like dark wetlands to Litney and Dokken. "In fact, we ought to turn off those lights and slow down. Those creatures might still be around."

Dokken and Litney turned off their flashlights and shoved them into their back pockets. They found a thicket to hunker down behind. Current crouched beside them. "Do you smell anything?" Litney asked the dog, all her senses straining.

"No, but then I didn't smell them the first time they were here."

"Do you hear anything?" Dokken asked.

"No, because we're talking," the dog muttered.

The three sat quietly, listening. The wind rustled the grass every now and again, and a few frogs chirped in the night, but the only out-of-place sound any of them could hear was a humming noise far over to their right. "That must be the interstate," Litney whispered. "I don't hear anything else, though."

"Neither do I," agreed the dog. "Let's move in nice and slow."

As she followed the dog toward the buildings, the moon broke through the clouds for a moment. When she saw Current in front of her, Litney could hardly believe how low the dog was to the ground. He crawled absolutely silently, his black-and-white body looking like it was coiled so tightly that it was only seconds away from blowing apart. Litney doubted she had ever been so intent on anything in her entire life.

When they reached the house, they saw the front door hanging open, swinging in the gentle breeze. The three of them peered inside. With the help of the flashlights, they saw the beautiful table and the benches had all been knocked over. One chair had even been shattered into pieces. Litney hadn't noticed the desk in the corner on their first visit, but now it was hard to miss since all of its drawers had been pulled out and its papers scattered like snowflakes all over the floor.

"These creatures were serious," Litney said, unable to keep the tremor out of her voice. "Talmoon and Pansy were not the only things they wanted. Obviously they were after something else."

"We should go back. We can't do this. We need to get help," Dokken said, backing away from the assaulted room toward the door. He was finding it hard to breathe. "We can go back to my house, get a good night's sleep and then talk this over in the morning. Because, really, what can we do tonight anyway? No one's here. We don't know where they've gone, and to be honest I don't want to know where they've gone. Come on. Let's go." He tugged at Litney's sleeve.

"Dokken," she said, pulling her arm away gently. "I'm scared, too, but Talmoon and Pansy need our help. We can't just abandon them."

"But, Litney, come on. Be serious. We can't do anything," Dokken argued. "What in the world can we do?"

Litney bent down and said to Current, "What do you think?"

"Come with me," the dog said, turning and trotting away.

"Where's he going now?" asked Dokken, clearly loathe to follow.

"I don't know," Litney said. She had taken a step in the direction of Current when she felt his hand on her sleeve again.

"Look," Dokken said, "I don't know what I was like on the last adventure, but I'm afraid I'm not so keen on this one. It's like *you* said. These creatures are serious."

"I know," Litney answered, making eye contact with Dokken but still trying to keep Current in her peripheral vision.

"So why aren't *you* scared?" he demanded.

"I am."

"No, *you're* not. Or at least not as scared as I am."

"You don't remember last time. There were lots of times when I was sure I was going to fail. When I was terrified. But it's the right thing to do, Dokken. That's what last time taught me. Even if I'm afraid, even if I think I'm going to fail, I want to be the kind of person who does something because it's the right thing to do."

"But why us? We should get real help," he repeated.

"Normally, I would agree. But Current said 'creatures.' And he also said Pansy mentioned we had the magic about us. That means that maybe having magic is important, that the 'normal authorities' wouldn't be much help in this situation." She feared she was going to have to leave Dokken standing there. Current had nearly disappeared from sight.

"Okay," he said as he ran a shaky hand over the bottom of his face. "Let's do this."

The dog had stopped and was waiting for them in front of the very barn where they had first heard Talmoon's voice, where Pansy had urged them to go explore in order to see Talmoon's gift. Even though Litney and Dokken knew that Talmoon was not there (which was the very reason the two of them were here), they still felt as if the man would appear out of nowhere and bark at them. That's why they moved more slowly than they needed to be moving.

When she got close enough so that she could whisper, Litney asked the dog, "What are we looking for in here?"

"When they were done ransacking the house, a bunch of the creatures came out here. Oh!" the dog exclaimed.

"What?" Litney and Dokken both asked at the same time.

"I forgot. There was a man with them. After all of the creatures had left, the man stayed here. He walked around the barn a couple of times. Then he went in through there," Current pointed at a low door that was surprisingly small for a barn, "but he came right back out. There's a second door inside, and Talmoon keeps that locked tight. The man wouldn't have been able to get in. But when he came back out, he circled the barn a couple more times, his hands behind his back and this odd smile on his face."

The dog howled.

"What are you thinking?" Dokken asked, and when the dog started rubbing his face along the grass and snorting, he decided this was the weirdest dog that had ever lived.

The dog stilled. "I could smell his scent on the breeze, and that man smelled . . . familiar."

"You mean you knew him?" Litney asked.

"No—" the dog answered. Then suddenly, he whispered, "Shhh, I hear something."

Litney and Dokken strained to hear whatever it was the dog thought he had heard. They couldn't make out anything except what they had heard before—the weeds blowing in the breeze, frogs chirping down in the swamp, and distant traffic. "Are you sure?" Litney whispered after a while.

The dog didn't answer, but they could hear him sniffing the air. "There's someone here—that same man!" Before they could respond to that news, Litney and Dokken found themselves snared at the waist as a big arm grabbed each of them.

Litney and Dokken both yelped while a deep voice said with relish, "Gotcha!"

Current began to bark and growl madly, and Litney worried that if the dog started biting, he might mistakenly bite her or Dokken. She shouted, "Let us go!" then kicked hard at her assailant's knee.

"Ouch!" the deep voice roared, and Litney fell to the ground, free. She scrambled around behind the man and after clasping her hands together, almost as if holding an invisible bat, she chopped at the middle of the man's back. Her father had told her the kidneys were back there somewhere and if you hit them, it could flatten someone instantly.

Which was exactly what happened. The man fell, and in his pain, he let Dokken go. Now that Litney and Dokken were free, the dog showed every single one of his sharp teeth and started to growl loudly, as if getting ready to attack. Even though his entire body was primed for it, Current did nothing. That's because a soft, but very scary, sound stopped him and everyone else. It was the sound of a gun being cocked. No one was sure where it was pointed. No one wanted to find out.

"You two are mighty strong," a man's deep voice said. "Guess I underestimated ya'll. I won't make that mistake again. Just as I wouldn't recommend you underestimating me. Understand?" The man climbed to his feet and while he wasn't as big as Talmoon, he was still huge.

"You're Talmoon's brother, aren't you?" Dokken asked, figuring that's why the man had smelled familiar to Current.

"Well, I certainly ain't Pansy's," the man said, and he found this so funny, he snorted. "Yeah. I'm his younger brother, Gunner."

Dokken laughed a weird nervous laugh.

"What's so funny?" the man with the gun asked in a way that told Dokken he was not supposed to be laughing.

Dokken cleared his throat and tried to get rid of the giggles that he could barely contain. He was scared to death, so how could he be laughing? "Sorry. It's just your name."

"You really want to be making fun of my name right now?"

"No, sir. It's just your name. It's Gunner. And you, you're holding a gun. It's funny." He started to laugh again, almost hysterically. It sounded very odd in the otherwise quiet night, very odd because he was the only one laughing. Dokken knew he had to stop himself. He had to stop this right now and get himself under control. He cleared his throat again, apologized again, and took a deep breath. Luckily, the giggles seemed to be gone.

"So . . . I'll bet ya'll are wondering what's going on. Where your precious Talmoon and Pansy are."

"You've got it all wrong. We hardly know them. We only met them once, and Pansy served us cookies and lemonade. She told us about Talmoon's pottery, but Talmoon wanted us to leave and never come back and we wouldn't have come back, except . . . I mean, we were just getting ready to head back home when you surprised us," Dokken prattled on and on before he could stop himself. It wasn't like he wanted to talk. Everything in his head was yelling at his mouth to keep quiet, but somehow his mouth had a mind of its own.

"Anybody ever tell you you should learn how to keep your trap shut?"

"Yes, sir. Many people, sir. Yes."

"Now would be a good time to learn that skill, got it?"

"Ye—" Dokken clamped a palm over his mouth and nodded. Since it was mostly dark, he doubted anyone could see him, but that was okay.

"Now, Pansy and Talmoon have something I want. No, that's not right. They have something I *need.* Meaning I *have* to have it. It's imperative that I get it. Do you understand?"

Neither Litney nor Dokken answered.

"Do you understand?" the man bellowed.

"Yes, sir. Yes. Yes, sir," the two of them sputtered.

"May I speak, sir?" Litney raised her hand as if she were in school.

"What?" the man demanded.

When Litney realized how silly it was to have her hand raised, she quickly lowered it and said, "Dokken wasn't lying, sir. We don't know them well. If you couldn't find what you were looking for, we certainly won't be able to help. Like Dokken said, we've only been out here once before, and that wasn't for very long, what with Talmoon wanting us to leave."

"Just like Talmoon to run you off. Even after all this time, he hasn't changed a bit. I don't know why she chose him," Gunner muttered to himself so quietly.

Litney had to ask, "What did you say?"

"Nothin'."

It occurred to Litney that the moon must have cleared itself of all clouds, because it felt brighter now. She was able to see Gunner and how much he looked like his brother, except for his hair. Whereas Talmoon had rich brown hair, Gunner's was almost completely silver, and it shone in the moonlight. This surprised Litney because Gunner had said he was Talmoon's *younger* brother. Something else that Litney noticed in the stronger moonlight was the glass bottle the man pulled out of his jacket. He unscrewed the top, took a long drink, and then repeated, "Yep. It's imperative."

"So why don't you get it yourself?" Dokken asked.

"What?" the big man asked, as if startled.

More slowly Dokken repeated his thought, "If it is so important, so imperative, why don't you go get whatever it is you need? Then we could just go home and—"

Gunner didn't just move, he pounced on Dokken, grabbing the kid by the back of the neck. "I don't know how many times I have to tell you, boy, but you'd better watch your mouth. You'll quit asking your little questions, and you'll do what I tell you. Got it?"

Dokken didn't respond.

Gunner shook Dokken and roared, "Got it?"

"Yes, yes, sir." Dokken's words tripped over themselves as they came out of his mouth. "We'll do whatever you tell us to, sir. I promise."

4

YOU CAN'T BE SERIOUS," Litney said, her voice quivering.

"You have no idea how serious I am," Gunner replied as Litney struggled to keep her balance. This was difficult since she was perched on the edge of the huge stone well that was located behind Talmoon's and Pansy's house. Gunner pointed the gun into the gaping dark mouth of the well. "Get down there"

"But we'll fall . . . we'll die," Litney pleaded.

"No, you won't. Now jump."

"We don't even know if there's water in there," Dokken piped up. He was squatting on the other side of the well, and his voice squeaked not from puberty, as it so often did these days, but from fear.

"You jump, and then you find Talmoon and Pansy, and you get what I need."

A phone started to ring. At first Dokken had thought it was his, but then Gunner stepped away from them for a moment and said, "Hello?"

Dokken knew he needed to talk to Litney while he had the chance. "Litney, I can't do this," he told her.

"I don't want to do it either," she whispered harshly.

"No. It isn't that. I know now why I'm so afraid."

"Because there's a man with a gun telling us to jump down a well and we don't know how deep it is or even if it has water in it. And if we do manage to survive the fall, who knows how we'll be able to get back out again."

"Duh, yes. But I mean before. I'm not a coward. I realized if I do this, I die."

"What are you talking about?" Litney demanded. "If you stay here, he'll shoot you and you surely will die."

"Last time," Dokken declared, exasperated because he didn't know if he'd have time to explain, and he needed Litney to understand what was upsetting him. He couldn't bear the idea that she might think him a coward. "The last time we went on a grand adventure—a grand adventure I don't even remember, by the way—I died. I died, Litney. I don't want to die again. I'm afraid if we go on another adventure, I'll die again. And I'm scared if I die this time, I won't come back. That's why I want to go home. I want to get someone else to help Talmoon and Pansy. Someone whose job it is to help people. Like the police, the sheriff or the FBI. They can do something."

Gunner, who had obviously finished his phone call, snarled, "Shut your traps and get down that well." He gave Litney a shove. She hung there for a moment, her hands grabbing wildly at the air, and then she was gone.

As Litney fell, she was sure she would hear Dokken any second now, screaming his way down behind her. When she continued to fall in silence, though, she grew more afraid. Maybe Gunner had only pushed her. Maybe she was going to have to do this all alone. That's why she thought, "Man, I sure wish I had the bracelet. At least then I would know I had some sort of power and protection." It also occurred to her that if she was falling down into the center of the hot earth (since she obviously wasn't just dropping to the bottom of a well), then she ought to be growing warmer, not colder. But that wasn't the case at all. What began as mild shivers shimmying around her body soon turned into huge trembling quakes, and Litney worried her fingers were getting so close to frozen that if they bumped against anything, they would simply shatter off.

It was when the tunnel began to grow all white with bright light that Litney knew she was nearing the end of her fall. She slid out onto some sort of ground or floor that was slick. As if she were on a newly Zambonied ice rink, she shot across this floor and slammed into a body. She had started to say, "I'm sorry," when a large whooping alarm began to shriek around her, cutting off any sound she might try to make.

If only her eyes could adjust, she thought, as she covered her ears to try and keep out the horrible noise. Her eyes burned because they felt as if she was looking directly at the sun—there was so much light around her. It wasn't only white light—although there was plenty of that—it was all kinds of light. Red and blue and green and flashing and pulsing and throbbing and with the siren screaming at her, all Litney could do was clamp her eyes shut, curl her body into a ball and try to protect her overwhelmed senses.

"Litney?" she heard a voice say behind her, but she could barely hear it because of all the racket. "What's going on?"

She opened one eye a slit and saw Dokken a couple of feet away in almost the same pose. Thank goodness he was here. "I don't know," she shouted, so she could be heard over the noise.

"Where are we?"

She didn't have time to answer. Something grabbed her by the armpits and started carrying her like she was a smelly baby. She twisted around to see what was holding her. Since it had a head that was some sort of cross between a human's and a falcon's, Litney was surprised when she didn't see any wings on the creature's back. And she was surprised that the feathers ended in a gorgeous mantle right at the neck. Just like Current had said, the body was covered in fur, and it was the color of a dark red wine that looked as if it was as soft as a rabbit's. The creature had legs that looked as powerful as a racehorse's, and if the grip under her arms was any indication, it also had large and strong hands. Litney thought the creature was so beautiful and noble looking that she didn't mind it was carrying her somewhere—she was sure it wouldn't cause her any harm.

The same could not be said for Dokken, however. The alarm had quit blaring, so Litney could hear him bellowing, "What are you doing? Put me down! I said put . . . me . . . down!" The thing carrying him—that had roasted-marshmallow colored fur—didn't respond, except to grab him around the waist and put a large hand over Dokken's mouth.

This place sure looked like earth, Litney thought to herself as the creature carried her to wherever it was taking her, but at the same time it wasn't like the earth she knew at all. When she glanced down, she saw she was being carried over what appeared to be a sidewalk. Not only was it the right color, it also had lines in it, just like the sidewalk Litney had walked on to get to her elementary school every day when she had been young. There were even green things in the cracks, like weeds growing. But it wasn't a sidewalk and those weren't weeds and that wasn't grass butting up against the sidewalk even though it, too, was green. Litney realized what the difference was. At home, the sidewalk was a sidewalk, the weeds were weeds, and the grass was grass. This stuff just looked like sidewalk and weeds and grass. It was almost as if they were traveling across a gigantic television screen and below their feet wasn't real cement or grass, only a brightly lit picture of cement and grass. It was the weirdest feeling—it was as if she was watching a television show of grass.

It was this strange everywhere. Over to her right they passed what was obviously supposed to be a tree, except this tree didn't have a round trunk or individual green leaves like every other tree Litney had ever seen. The trunk on this tree was cardboard flat, it glowed brown, and the leaves, if you could call them that, were simply a long thin tube of neon green wrapped around and around into a big circle. The tree looked like a big lollipop. Before long the green light of the leaves started to flash, then light began to dash madly through the circles. Finally a rainbow raced around the tubing until the entire thing eventually went back to being a solid green.

What else was different? There didn't seem to be any cars or bikes or motorcycles, but some of the creatures around them appeared to be moving faster than the others. Litney realized some creatures were standing on a sort of conveyor belt just like she had seen at airports. Litney loved riding on those while her father walked on the normal ground beside her on the way to their plane. Her father would get to walking so fast (since the rule was he couldn't run to beat her) that his butt would start to do this wild wiggle thing. Litney usually ended up winning those races, probably because her father always carried a heavy bag with his computer and papers weighing him down. But what struck Litney now was that whether these creatures were moving quickly on the conveyor belts or moving more slowly on the sidewalks, no one spoke to anyone else. No one even looked at anyone else. Everyone seemed as if they had some place very important they had to get to and no one dared take a moment, not even a second, to be interested in the other people or the surroundings around them.

Tink, tink, tink, Litney heard as she felt her body come to a stop. The creature had knocked on what looked like a door in the middle of a wall on the bottom of a building, but it wasn't a door on a wall of a building at all. The door that opened looked like a wooden door, but when Litney examined it, she saw the door was really made of glass and quite thin—like a shower door. Obviously the brown, the wood, the entire door-ness was being projected into or through this piece of glass. That's probably what was going on with everything she had seen. Her television screen idea had been right.

"Thank you, Carriers," a voice that almost sounded British said. The voice belonged to another one of the creatures, although this one had a face that looked like it was half bird, half woman, and it added, "You may put them in the drawing room."

Litney and Dokken were carried inside and plopped on what appeared to be a nice soft sofa, but because it was made of glass like everything else seemed to be, they landed on it with a hard thunk. "Ouch!" Dokken said, rubbing his elbow.

"I know," Litney agreed as she felt the sofa bite into the back of her body with its sharp edges.

Now that they had deposited the two kids, the two bird-headed creatures turned and left without a word. After several unsuccessful tries of sitting on the hard, slippery couch without falling off, both Litney and Dokken decided to stand.

The new creature—whose fur was a rich navy-blue—approached, and the way it looked at her gave Litney an immediate case of the creeps. It was looking at Litney like she was somewhere between dinner and a worm. "Good afternoon, kind master and miss," the creature said. "What a grand pleasure it is to make your acquaintance. My name is Miss Bootlicker. Might I interest you in some tea?"

Was this thing for real? Litney knew she wasn't in her own world, but no one spoke like that, did they? It reminded her of the characters she had watched in *Pride and Prejudice*. Litney had never had the time or patience for manners and "might I's" and "Misses," and all she wanted to do right now was blurt out, "What in the heck's going on?" But this thing, whatever it was, seemed to be doing its best to sound all British and proper. Litney somehow sensed that if she wanted to get any information about where they were or why they were there, she probably needed to match this creature's manners. She said, "Yes, please. Tea would be lovely. My friend, Master Dokken, would also appreciate a cup as well. Perhaps after we have received our tea, you might be so kind as to tell us where we are and what it is we may do for you."

Dokken gaped at her like two green arms had just climbed out of her nostrils and started waving at him.

The creature inclined its head toward Litney in a gesture that could have been admiration or respect, and then it clapped together its oversized hands. At first, both Dokken and Litney assumed they were waiting for someone else to enter the room with the tea things. It wasn't until a few moments had passed that they realized two long golden strands on the chandelier above them were now snaking their way downward. Their descent was a dance, a slither, a twirl, and when the golden strands got closer, Litney and Dokken could see two teacups were hooked onto one of them. Miss Bootlicker gently lifted the cups off, a surprising feat given the size of her hands, and put one of them beneath the second golden strand. With a quiet *psssssssh*, a thin flow of water streamed out into the first cup and then the other. "Would you like cream or sugar?" Miss Bootlicker inquired.

"Nah," Dokken said, and then added quickly after a look from Litney, "I mean, no thank you, Miss Bootlicker."

"I do not wish to have any either, thank you," Litney said.

"Won't you please sit?" Miss Bootlicker gestured toward the impossible sofa. Dokken watched as Litney slowly lowered herself down on the seat and managed to stay there. He followed and found that if he didn't lean back, he could pretty much stay where he was. "Here you go," the creature said as she handed them their tea.

"Thank you," they murmured. Both of them took polite sips, and Dokken was about to exclaim, "But it's only water!" when Litney glared at him with a look that told him to not say a word. It was becoming more and more obvious to her that this world was all about appearances. Things weren't real. They only appeared real.

"Do you find the tea to your liking?" Miss Bootlicker asked, fluffing the ring of feathers around her neck.

"Mmmm. It is so clear and crisp," Litney replied with a forced smile, when, in reality, the tepid water almost made her gag. "Just what we needed."

"That's wonderful. Well, I must say it is such a pleasure to have you stopping by for a visit this afternoon," Miss Bootlicker said, and Litney had to stop herself from saying something snide, like neither she nor Dokken had been given much of a choice. "But perhaps it is time to come to the point of our little gathering, yes?"

"That would be lovely," Litney said. She thought about crossing her legs, but decided that might upset the precarious balance she had managed on the sofa. She sat a little straighter and looked directly at Miss Bootlicker's disturbing eyes.

"You are in the land of Gad, which of course makes me a Gadlander. My king needs your assistance." Miss Bootlicker paused, and Litney swore that if the Gadlander had been wearing a dress, she would have smoothed her large hands along her skirts. When the pause lengthened, it was obvious the creature was trying to find the best words for what she wanted to say next. "My king has recently . . . entertained . . . some friends of yours."

"Entertained, my butt. You mean kidnapped," Dokken muttered. Litney heard him and knew this could potentially upset Miss Bootlicker, but Dokken was right. There were no ifs, ands, or buts about it: Pansy and Talmoon had been kidnapped.

Miss Bootlikcer might have heard what he said and she might not have. Regardless, she soldiered on. "These friends of yours have something that is of utmost importance to my king. To all of us here in Gad. It is imperative that you help us in this matter."

Like the bracelet had been of the utmost importance to Mala, Litney thought as she narrowed her eyes. "What is it your king would like us to do? We hardly know the two people of whom you speak. I am not sure we can be of any assistance." Litney found herself thinking of Mr. Michaels, her sixth-grade teacher who had pounded grammar and all its rules about indirect objects and adjectival clauses and "whos" and "whoms" into her head for nine very long months. She had hated him then, but as this formal conversation continued, she had never been gladder for a teacher's obsession and nitpickiness.

"Oh, but we think you *can* help us. In fact, let us go right now and see Talmoon. He will be able to give you a sense of how . . . urgent this is." Miss Bootlicker was fast. She was almost out of the room before Dokken and Litney had even stood up.

They followed the creature down a hall, around a corner, up some stairs, around another corner and then down some stairs. Litney hoped Dokken was paying attention to which way they were going, because if they had to run out of here in some mad dash for escape, she didn't think she could remember which way to go.

A RAT.

That's what Talmoon looked like as Litney and Dokken stood above his room and stared down at him. The room he was in had no ceiling, and it was long and narrow, like a hospital hallway. Its walls glowed a sickly green, as if every square inch of them had been covered in vomit-colored light bulbs.

As Talmoon paced relentlessly from one end of the room to the other, it was impossible not to notice the floor beneath him. It was a checkerboard of neon colors—green, red, pink, yellow, and blue—but the rampant range of colors didn't stay put in their squares. Instead, the different colors jumped from square to square. Sometimes the entire thing flashed and flickered, and sometimes only a single square did a hyper-strobe. Within less than a minute of looking at the floor, Litney thought she was going to be sick. All that moving light made her body feel as if it was rocking and roiling on some small boat in the worst storm. How could Talmoon stand it?

"Talmoon!" Dokken shouted down. "Are you okay?" He was no longer afraid of the big man. He was so upset by what he saw that all he wanted to do was help.

Talmoon stopped his pacing to look up. Even though he looked like some ferocious caged beast, wild wasn't the best word that could be used to describe his eyes. Unhinged was probably closer.

"Get me outta here!" His voice was hard, but hoarse, as if escaping was the water that would save his thirsty soul.

"Good afternoon, Mr. Strange," Miss Bootlicker called down to him. She even waved. "So lovely to see you again."

"Go to h—-"

"I have your friends here with me," Miss Bootlicker interrupted him, but her tone stayed as light as a June breeze. "We have brought them to see you, but I must warn you. This is not a pleasure visit. We wanted them to see you so they could know just how very important it is that they help us locate the item my king so desperately desires."

"Don't bring them into this. Send them back. Now!"

Miss Bootlicker laughed as if the man had just said something flirty to her. As she did so, the feathers on her head trembled and fluttered. When everything had smoothed back down, she continued. "I fear that simply is not possible. So, I need you to tell them where to find it."

"No."

Neither Litney nor Dokken were sure how she made this happen because Miss Bootlicker hadn't moved a muscle, but as soon as that word was out of Talmoon's mouth, the entire floor swelled and heaved and rolled with color. Not only that, but a high-pitched whine also filled the room. Talmoon clamped his eyes shut to block out the light, but, even with his hands over his ears, the noise felled him to one knee.

"Stop, please," Litney begged the tall creature. "You're hurting him."

"My dear, how can I be hurting him?" she asked, her golden eyes glittering as she watched the man below them. "Do you see any marks? Any blood?"

"That's absurd!" Dokken shouted. "It's obvious you're hurting him. Stop it. Stop it now!"

Everything stopped. The floor went dull and dark gray, like a television screen turned off, and the walls did the same. Slowly, Talmoon peeled his hands away from his ears, opened his eyes and stood up.

"Mr. Strange. I am sending these two into the room with you."

"No!" Litney shouted, startling even herself with how sharply she had said this. "We . . . we can't go in that room." She would do what she could to save Talmoon, but there was no way they were going to get her in that room. It was a nightmare.

"Oh, dear," Miss Bootlicker said with a laugh. "I am not asking you to stay in that room as we have asked Mr. Strange to stay there. I am inviting you to join him so that he can tell you what you need to find for us and where it is. I will return in fifteen minutes. That will certainly be enough time for you to have a lovely conversation. Ta-ta." Miss Bootlicker sauntered down the hall on her long powerful legs.

A space opened in the railing they had been standing behind, and some stairs slid out from the wall and went all the way down into the room. Escape for all three of them might have been possible if it weren't for the two Gadlanders standing behind them with what looked like huge hypodermic needles filled with glowing blue liquid. Litney and Dokken were sure they didn't want to find out what was in there.

The two of them descended the stairs, and it wasn't until they were at the bottom that they were reminded of how big Talmoon was. From up above, he had looked like a normal man, but standing in front of him once again, he towered over them. Plus, now he had those wild eyes to add to the equation, all of which equaled terrifying.

"Pansy?" the man whispered. "Are they doing this to her?"

"We don't know. We don't know where she is," Litney said, wishing she had a different answer, because she was afraid this might be what would send him over the edge.

"You have no idea what it's like," Talmoon said, but he didn't look at them. It seemed as if he was talking to the wall. Litney wasn't sure how this could be the case, but the man standing before them suddenly seemed weak and even small.

"Can we help? I mean, we can get them what they need and give it to them, so we can get you two out of here." Dokken said. "Just tell us what it is and where we can find it, and we'll be right back with it. We'll have you out of here in no time. You and Pansy."

Talmoon didn't answer. He had started pacing again. "But how did you two get here? I don't understand."

"Current came to get us," Litney answered. "Then we went to the farm. Your brother was there. He pushed us down the well, and we ended up here."

Talmoon froze the instant Litney said the word "brother." "Gunner?" When the name came out, it was strangled in a way that made Litney and Dokken step closer together. Talmoon ran a shaking hand through his hair. Then he shook his head and gave one of those kinds of laughs that wasn't a laugh at all. "Of course."

If Litney and Dokken thought that "of course" meant Talmoon would fill them in on all of this, they were wrong. By the time Miss Bootlicker had returned, they had tried everything they could think of to get him to talk. But they knew nothing more about what it was they were looking for or where they would find it than when she had left.

"How disappointing," Miss Bootlicker murmured as she escorted the two kids back up the stairs, leaving Talmoon and his distressed eyes to face the narrow walls and flashing lights all alone.

5

As they left Talmoon alone in his cell and followed Miss Bootlicker back to the room with the hard couch, they heard her murmuring, "I need that liquid. I was certain he would tell me what it was when I brought these kids to him. The king will be furious." The tightness in her voice made Litney think Miss Bootlicker was either very furious or very afraid. "What do I do now? It's obvious these two don't know anything, so throwing them in a cell won't do anything. Maybe if I send them back, they'll be able to find it. Yes, that's what I'll do. Because they must find it. They *must.*" Her monologue ceased as they entered the first room they had been brought to, and Miss Bootlicker rang some kind of a buzzer. Two creatures appeared and after skewering the two kids with her eyes, she said, "I want you to remember Talmoon in that room. Remember how horrible it is."

"But what can we do?" Litney cried. "We tried to get it out of him."

The creature shrugged and smiled a horrible smile, one that seemed to say she would have a delightful time continuing to torture the poor man. Then she gave a general kind of gesture, something along the lines of "Get them out of here." The creatures dragged Litney and Dokken back to the place where they had come sliding out onto the floor.

"What does she expect us to do?" Litney asked.

Dokken shrugged. "For me, the bigger question is how are we going to get back home? We slid down and out."

Litney shook her head. The two creatures didn't answer either, only herded them onto a black circle. Some button must have been pressed, because the circle started to rise off the floor. When Litney and Dokken looked up to figure out where they were going, they saw a tube above them. The circle they had been standing on fit into the bottom of the tube, and when it locked into place, it was like a huge vacuum hose had been put on top of them. In an instant, they were whisked up and away from Gad.

The trip back was just as cold, but this time Litney was tightly holding Dokken's hand, so it didn't seem as bad. At the same time, it was even worse, because she was touching Dokken. As they dropped (or flew, she wasn't sure which verb applied), she couldn't see him, probably because her eyes were squeezed shut, but she could feel his hand holding strongly onto her own. It comforted her, sure, but she couldn't help thinking about the conversation she'd had on the swing with her grandfather. "There is always a boy who goes along," he had said—and he had admitted he had been the boy who had gone along with her grandmother, and her father had been the boy who had gone along with her mother.

Wait a minute! Litney remembered now. Her mother had said the same thing. On the day she had received the bracelet, as they had been packing to go to her grandparents' farm, her mother had said something about the bracelet bringing her Litney's father. This must have been what she meant. But to marry Dokken? She liked him a lot, but he was so . . . so orange. If they got married and had a baby girl and she came out as orange-ly as Dokken, she'd have to name the poor girl Clementine, like the tiny oranges she loved eating all winter long. But would that be so bad? He was kind and sort of cute with all that red hair and all those freckles and—

A panicked, "Oh, no!" from Dokken interrupted her thoughts as her body began to scrape against something. The rocks from the well. His concern was the fact that as soon as their heads had crested the mouth of the well, the two of them had started to fall back down instead of up. He managed to grab onto the side of the well just in time to keep himself from falling. Litney hadn't been quick enough to do the same, and now the only thing keeping her from crashing back down into the black was the fact that she was holding onto Dokken's other hand. "Can you pull us up?" she asked in a tone that almost sounded like a plea.

He grunted some. "No. I can't budge us at all. Not that that's surprising. I can't even do a pull-up with only myself in gym class. Oh, gosh!"

She didn't have to ask what had prompted this exclamation—she had felt his hand slip so that the two of them dropped lower into the black pit of the well. "What are we going to do?" she asked.

"Think, Dokken," the boy muttered to himself. "Think! Okay, are there any stones sticking out where your feet are? Can you find anything to stand on?"

She felt around with her feet. Nothing. Nope. Nothing. There. "Yes! I've found one!" She had never been so glad to have small feet in her life. She managed to squeeze both of them onto a rock that jutted out some like a little shelf, and after she had done that, she heard Dokken sigh in relief.

"Oh, that's much better," he said. "Can you balance there?"

"I think so. Why?"

"Because if you can let go of my hand, I can try and swing it up to the ledge. Then if you could help me by giving a little shove, I think I can get up."

"But, but that leaves me down here," she said, uncertainly.

"I know, but then I can go find a rope or something and pull you up."

"But that leaves me down here," she repeated.

"It's the only thing I can think of. Otherwise both of us will stay stuck down here. Do you have any better ideas?"

Darnit. No. "Okay, fine. Just hurry. Please. Hurry." She got as balanced as she could on the little shelf, and then she put a hand under one of Dokken's shoes. When he counted to three, she pushed while he pulled. It took some work, but finally he hoisted himself up and out of the hole.

"Hurry. Please," she said, and even though it had only been a whisper, the word please seemed to echo off the rocks around her.

"WHAT TOOK YOU SO LONG, Dokken Carver?" Litney demanded when a thick rope with a big knot on the end dropped down into the well and bonked her on the nose. "I told you to hurry." As she had waited and shivered in that dark dank well, she had decided she was going to punch him in the arm when she got to the top. She grabbed tightly onto the rope and felt herself pulled out of the well as easily as if she were a rag doll. Maybe Dokken was stronger than he thought.

Or maybe Dokken stood over there with his hands tied behind his back, and it was Gunner who had pulled her up. "So he didn't tell you a thing, huh?" the man asked, leaning his face close into hers. He was obviously hoping to get a different answer from her than he had from Dokken.

"No, sir. I'm sorry."

"That's too bad for him and Pansy. And for you."

"But we did what we could!" Dokken exclaimed when Litney came to stand beside him. Gunner quickly tied her hands behind her back as well. "He wouldn't even tell us what it was you all wanted, let alone where we could find it."

"I can tell you what we all want, but then it's up to you to find it. I'll come back in three days, and if you don't have it . . . well, let's just say you don't want that to be the case. Now," the big man said as he bent over and scratched his leg. "I'm looking for something important."

Both of the kids waited to hear what it was, this obviously important thing, but Gunner didn't say anything else. "We know it's important, sir," Dokken said, trying to keep the impatience out of his voice and only barely succeeding. "But what is it?"

"Well, I'm not entirely sure. It has something to do with liquid. Or making liquid. And the liquid can do a kind of magic thing."

"What do you mean you aren't exactly sure?" Litney asked.

"And it has something to do with liquid? And it can do magic? That isn't much help," Dokken added, wishing he could have been even more honest so he could say that was the stupidest thing he had ever heard.

"That's all I can tell you," the man growled. "Be glad you have that much. I said three days. And I'll be back."

"But, sir, wouldn't it make more sense for you to look for this?" Litney asked. "You at least have some idea of what you are looking for."

Gunner looked over his shoulder at the house. "I can't stay here," he spat out. "Their perfect little house. Their perfect little farm. It makes me want to take a match to it all. But if I did that, well, then I couldn't find what I was looking for, could I? That's why you have to do it. And you will do it because you're good, nice kids. And if you don't do it, you good nice kids will have to live with the fact that you allowed two people to suffer and maybe even die. And I wouldn't think about getting other people involved if I were you. That'll only make things take longer, and who knows how long those creatures will keep my brother and Pansy alive. Could you live with that? I don't think so. So get busy."

Litney and Dokken watched Gunner disappear into the dark gray that comes a little bit before dawn, and an irritated Dokken said, "Why in the heck did he tie us up if he was only going to leave?"

Litney started wriggling her hands in an attempt to get free. She shrugged. "That seems to be the least of our worries. Three days? How are we going to figure out what we're looking for and then find it all in three days? I remember thinking this as we were falling through the well the first time, but man, I wish I had the bracelet. And Asta. Asta could help us figure all of this out."

A deep growl followed by a snarl came from their right. The pre-dawn darkness and fog made it impossible to see. "Please tell me that was Current doing something weird," Dokken whispered.

"I don't think so," Litney replied, her eyes squinting into the gloom.

"So . . . what was it?"

The next sound they heard made Dokken even more frightened. The thing, whatever it was, started to grunt, and the grunting seemed to be getting closer. He fully expected a werewolf to emerge out of the fog and swallow him whole.

As soon as Litney heard the sound, however, relief and excitement flooded her voice. "Asta!"

"Who's there?" the voice asked in the thick gray darkness.

"Asta, it's me. Litney."

"No, it can't be."

"It is. Come this way and you'll see." Apparently Litney couldn't wait for the bear to make it to her, because she had started to run in the direction of Asta's voice, even though her hands were still tied behind her back.

"Oh, Litney. It is you!"

"Asta," Litney said as she lost herself in the furry hug of the bear. She had forgotten how strong and wild her bear smell was, but instead of feeling overpowered by the scent, it soothed her.

"I never thought I'd see you again," the bear said thickly.

"I know," Litney replied, turning and asking, "Can you help me get these off?" After a moment's work with her sharp teeth, the ropes fell to the ground in a heap.

"Ahem," Dokken cleared his throat.

"Who's that?" the bear snarled and stood on her hind legs.

"It's Dokken."

"Dokken?" the bear asked, stupefied. "But . . . he's dead. I-I helped bury him myself."

"See, Litney?" Dokken said, a strong sense of vindication coloring his voice. "I'm not the only one who thinks it's weird to be dead and then not dead."

The bear lumbered over to where Dokken stood. "Dokken, it is wonderful to see you again. How are you?"

When the body belonging to the rough voice emerged out of the morning mist, Dokken's eyes popped and his jaw sagged. It really was a bear, and a huge one at that. He shook himself and squeaked, "I-I'm good. Glad I'm not dead, you know?" He hoped he wasn't about to be dead again as Asta attacked the ropes on his wrists. When Dokken was free, he was relieved enough that he could continue in a more normal voice. "Well, good except for the fact that the two of us probably will be dead in three days."

"Why is that?" the bear asked, her voice tinged with alarm as she turned to gaze at Litney. "And by the way, do you have any idea how I am here now?"

"The answer to your first question will take awhile to answer," Litney said. "As to how you're here now, I think it happened because I wished you were here. You and the bracelet." She looked down and whispered, "Oh, my."

"What?" Dokken and Asta asked at the same time.

Litney tentatively held up her right hand—the bracelet shone from her wrist like the moon.

"I THINK WE SHOULD GO HOME," Litney said as the sun pushed its way into the sky and she brushed the hair out of her eyes. They had just finished telling Asta all that had occurred up to this point, and the bear had sat patiently, listening and "Hmmmmming," now and again.

This statement from Litney surprised Dokken. It's what he had wanted to say more than anything since they had gotten out of the well, but he had held his tongue because he was tired of being the one who was always afraid.

"We need to get sleep and food," Litney added to clarify why she was urging them to go home.

"There's food here. As for sleep, we don't have much time," Current said as he circled Asta for what seemed like the thousandth time. Current had reappeared only after Gunner had left, probably thinking everything was safe and clear—that was until he saw that a mammoth bear had come into his yard.

"Would you stop running around me?" growled the bear. "You're making me dizzy."

The dog slowed, but did not stop. It was almost as if his body couldn't stop, because standing in front of him was this big thing that made every instinctual fiber in his body kick into high alert. Current told Asta, "I think better when I'm moving."

"And I think better when I'm not annoyed," the bear replied, stretching to her full frightening height and flexing her paws. "Sit down. Now."

Current sat, but that didn't mean he was still. Before long, he had one of his hind feet in his mouth and was chewing his nails.

Asta eyed the dog, daring him to move again. When he didn't, except for continuing to bite his nails, the bear continued, "I agree with the nutjob dog. I think it's best you stay here. We don't have time to waste. We need to get working on this now, because all we have to go on is that we're looking for a magical liquid. That's not much to go on, especially if we have to find it in the next three days."

Despair rolled over the small group, but Litney's eyes brightened as she recalled a conversation she once had with her grandfather about his crazy great uncle Tobias. "Hey. Gunner said we were looking for a magical liquid. Or something that made a liquid magical. What if it's a still?"

"A what?" the dog asked, and the bear looked confused as well.

"A still!" Dokken said excitedly because now that Litney had said it, it made perfect sense. He explained, "I did a report on stills last year in social studies when we were studying the Eighteenth Amendment. Litney, do you mind if I tell them?"

Litney gestured in a way that said, "Be my guest."

"Do you know what alcohol is?" Dokken asked Current and Asta.

"Yes. It's a drink that can make people loopy," Current replied since he had seen Talmoon and Pansy dancing tipsily together after sharing a bottle of wine. Then the dog added, "Or dangerous. Pansy reads the newspaper sometimes, and she's always telling us about fights and accidents caused by alcohol."

Dokken nodded. "In the 1920s, the United States government passed the Eighteenth Amendment which pretty much made all alcohol illegal. But some people weren't about to go without it, so stills started popping up, usually in remote places like this. And stills were what people used to make homemade alcohol, or moonshine as they called it. Stills were usually made out of copper, and then they would mix it up and it would turn into alcohol somehow. I don't remember that part so well," Dokken said scratching his red head. "But then, after that was all done, they had to get the moonshine to the people who wanted it without getting caught by the authorities. That was called running."

He paused for a moment and thought this out more fully: back then, people were willing to do anything to run and buy moonshine. Why wouldn't the same be true here? They were, after all, in the middle of nowhere. What better place to have a still? And if those Gadlandians, or whatever they were, liked alcohol, then why couldn't that be what everyone was after? He finished, "I think you might be on to something, Litney. If we could just grab something to eat, then start poking around, we might be able to find what everyone's looking for pretty quickly. Then we can go home."

"I doubt it is going to be that easy," Asta said as she began to lumber toward the house, sniffing the ground as she went.

"Why not? It sounds plausible to me," Dokken countered as he followed the bear. "I know all about this. You can't even imagine what people like Al Capone were willing to do for moonshine."

"That might be true, but if it was that simple or obvious, the creatures who took your friends would have already found what they were looking for. I'll bet a still, whatever it is, is rather large. Pretty hard to hide something like that, don't you think?"

Dokken didn't answer the bear, and he knew he should probably listen to Asta, but instead he chose to pay attention to the hope that they would find a still so he could be safe and home by lunchtime.

THEY RESTORED THE KITCHEN TO SOME ORDER by putting the kitchen table and chairs back upright and picking up the papers. Then they grabbed some cold chicken from the icebox that did indeed have a big block of ice inside it and finished off some lemonade they found as well. It was an odd breakfast, but they couldn't find much else.

When they had cleaned up their dishes, there was not much debate over where they should start looking, which was why they now all stood staring into the infamous barn—the one Litney and Dokken had been peering into when Talmoon had found them, the one Gunner had circled after the others had come and taken Talmoon and Pansy away.

While it wasn't a huge barn like some that dotted the farms in the area, it did dwarf the rest of the buildings. Like the house, it had a base of stones—

each of them big enough to fill a kitchen sink if not half a bathtub. The wall of stones ended at the height of Litney's head, and then it became planks. These boards were not painted the usual red but had been stained dark. They reminded her of the forests described in fairy tales—a deep and foreboding black-brown. The doorway had the appearance of a black hole—no one could tell what they would be sucked into if they dared step inside.

"You go first," Litney suggested to Dokken, giving his shoulder a little push.

"No," he said, shrugging away from her. "Ladies first. I insist."

"That's absurd. I'll bet you've never said that in your entire life before."

"In fact I have," he countered with a smug smile. "Every time we've had to give reports in front of the class, I'm always a gentleman and let all the girls go first."

"And you do this out of the goodness of your heart?" she asked. "Not because you're a chicken who's afraid of public speaking or anything?"

"Would one of you get in there?" Asta exclaimed, her voice exasperated.

"If you're so anxious to go in there, why don't you go first?" Dokken retorted to the bear.

"Look at the door. Look at me. End of argument," the bear said flatly.

The bear was right. Though tall it was a peculiarly narrow door. "Fine. I'll go in," Litney said, with a huff. "I have the bracelet. Hopefully it'll help me see."

"It's about time," Asta muttered. "You'd think it was a lion's den the way you two are carrying on."

Litney held up her wrist and went in. The bracelet did glow, but only dimly, and the darkness was so thick that the meager light from her wrist did little to dispel it. She wanted to back out, but the disapproving look that was sure to appear on Asta's face stopped her. Plus, she didn't have time for fear. They only had three days to figure all of this out.

Since her bracelet was doing little to help her see, her next instinct was to walk over to a wall, hoping something there or on a shelf would help. At least then she could begin to feel her way around, maybe get her bearings. But when she took a first step, she tripped on the uneven floor and fell, scraping the palms of her hands on the bricks or stones that heaved and buckled underneath her. "Ouch!" she whispered harshly. She always hated scrapes like that, how they tore the skin right off. Yes, it was gross and unsanitary, but she couldn't stop herself—she put each of her palms in her mouth. This made the stinging worse, but only for a moment. And then the pain was gone. The taste of dirt in her mouth wasn't. She spat, spat again and wondered what to do.

"I wish I had more light," she murmured. Almost like Aladdin's lamp, the bracelet obliged. Light—wide and strong—filled the room, and she felt her shoulders relax in relief. Apparently the bracelet wanted her to be more specific. She'd have to remember that.

Looking around with the light provided by the bracelet, she realized this couldn't be the whole barn. This must be some sort of anteroom—some small, empty, dark and windowless entryway. In front of her stood another door, one so massive, it reminded her of the doors she had seen on churches. It was even peaked and pointed at the top. The door was covered almost entirely in a black wrought-iron sculpture. Litney stepped closer and saw the iron had been fashioned into everything from a flower and a branching tree to a full moon.

"It isn't going to open," she whispered, remembering that Current had said Talmoon kept it locked tight. She was right. When she tried pushing the handle down, it wouldn't budge. She held her bracelet up close to the handle, to see if there was some sort of keyhole. There wasn't. How in the world did this door open? What should she do? Go back outside and ask the others what they thought? Just as she was about to turn and leave, she wondered if she had to push some trick spot on the door. She started pressing things—the flower, the elephant, the tipi, the owl, and the pig. After pushing on nearly everything else, she decided to try the moon that was high up on the door, wondering if Talmoon had a sense of humor—a tall moon. Apparently he did, because she heard a click. The door swung open.

When she stepped inside the next room, she gasped, and every one of her senses jumped to life. Light streamed in through a line of windows that ran along the spine of the roof. The light hit the walls that were the same honey-colored wood as the table they had eaten at with Pansy. A glow blanketed the room, and it smelled wonderful.

But it wasn't only light pouring in here. It was also water. How had she not heard all the water falling out in the other room? It must have been that door or incredible sound proofing, because the outer room had been absolutely silent. But in here the sound of flowing water was as loud as if she stood in front of twenty small waterfalls. Long copper pipes, at least a dozen, ran from the floor all the way to the ceiling. Out of these copper pipes obviously came water, but the water didn't fall straight back down. Rather, it traveled through teapot after teapot set on platforms that had been attached to the copper pipes. These platforms and teapots circled around the pipes like spiral staircases. At the bottom of each of these pipes, the last teapot poured its water out into a wooden tub where water pooled and tiny koi swam beneath miniature green plants that blossomed with yellow flowers. That must be what she smelled. She closed her eyes and inhaled—the scent was sweet but with a little sadness at the end of it. When she opened her eyes, she reached out to put her hand in some falling water. The palm of her hand filled with the insistent liquid that was a little cooler than her skin, and the water felt smooth and charged at the same time. Oh, and was that a bird? Yes. A sun-yellow finch, and it had a nest. There. In the corner.

"This is the most beautiful place I've ever seen," Dokken said behind her. She jumped because she hadn't heard him come in. But that wasn't surprising with all this water flowing.

"Isn't it?" she agreed as she turned back to look at the room, seeing the finch fly up to the ceiling only to disappear out one of the windows that must have been open a crack.

"And look at these teapots," Dokken urged.

Litney had been so taken by the big scale, she had neglected to examine Talmoon's work more closely. The teapot Litney's parents had back at home in the cupboard was the same white as a toilet bowl, and plump as a cantaloupe. It was pleasant, but certainly not noteworthy. In fact, she never thought about the teapot again after her father had gotten done serving her some tea, which he did almost every morning when he was home. It was a little ritual the two of them shared. Her mother preferred coffee, but Litney and her father had been drinking tea and passing the comics back and forth between them every morning they were together for as long as she could remember. She loved this time with him. She missed it terribly when he traveled.

Nor were these teapots similar to the only other teapot Litney had ever used—the one at the Chinese restaurant on Minnesota Avenue. That one was small, slender and silver, much like the waitress who knew to give Litney chopsticks instead of a fork.

As Pansy had said, Talmoon's teapots were nothing like she had ever seen before—and their uniqueness did make her inhale with wonder. The pots all tended to be the same basic shape—a rounded square was the only way Litney could think to describe it, kind of like a marshmallow, but with corners. Then on that repeating form, Talmoon had played endlessly. One teapot had barely blue globules of glaze on it so that it looked like rain drops had beaded on the outside of the pot. Another was the color of dusty earth and then had what looked like fading shafts of wheat blown and bending because of some invisible wind. This one looked like a storm crossing a prairie. That one looked like the shadow of a tall pine.

"This could be a fancy kind of still," Dokken said hopefully as he walked over to one of the teapot waterfalls. He put a hand in the liquid like Litney had done, only he brought his cupped hand to his mouth to taste the liquid. "No," he said with a scowl. "Only water."

"But this place is important," she said. "It's got to be the key. Gunner told us we were looking for a liquid or something that made liquid magical." She surveyed the inside of the barn—everywhere was liquid and it sure felt magical. This had to be the place. "Current said Gunner came inside, but only for a moment. He probably didn't know how to open the big door."

"Speaking of, how did you open it?" Dokken asked.

"You push on the moon near the top," she told him. "Get it? Talmoon? It seemed obvious, especially after I'd pushed everything else."

He laughed. "That makes sense. Hey, if Gunner hadn't been able to open that door and make it in here, he wouldn't have known if this is what he was looking for. But maybe that doesn't matter—it's just water."

"This has to be what everyone's after, even though it tastes like water," Litney said, gesturing to the copper pipes around them. "How could it not?"

"Exactly," Dokken agreed. "Let's go see what the others think."

"No," THE DOG SAID WHEN THEY asked him if Gunner could have made it inside the barn. "He was in there only a few seconds."

"You're sure?" Litney asked. It was very important they be certain.

"I'm sure."

"Then this has to be it," Dokken exclaimed, finally ready to believe that they had figured out all they needed to figure out.

"Explain to me once more what's inside," Asta said as she looked into the girl's eyes.

Litney explained as quickly but accurately as she could, and when she finished speaking, she returned the bear's gaze. Then she asked. "What do you think? Is this what we're looking for?"

"It could be," Asta answered. "But I don't think we should stop looking at other possibilities just yet."

"Why not?" Dokken cried. "This is it. It has to be. It's liquid and it's magical. End of story."

"I said it could be," Asta said evenly, "but what's the harm in looking around a little more?"

"We want to get Talmoon and Pansy out of there. It was horrible," Litney said with urgency.

"I understand that," the bear said, nodding her great, furry head. "But you also want to make sure you're right, don't you? You don't want to waste precious time assuming you have what these people are looking for only to find out you don't." Asta paused to let her words sink in, before she concluded,"because then Talmoon and Pansy might never be released."

Dokken's frustration came out in a huge sigh. "But there's really no way we can know we're right unless we find Gunner and ask."

"All I'm saying," the bear replied, keeping her voice low and steady, "is that perhaps we ought to look around a little more to make sure. How about we give this three hours? After that, if you still feel certain that the water in the barn is the thing everyone is after, then we'll find a way to get Gunner back here. Deal?" She stuck out her huge, clawed paw toward Dokken.

He didn't want to shake her paw. He wanted to find Gunner right now. What would waiting three hours reveal? Nothing. He was certain of that. He glanced at Litney, hoping she was feeling the same way he was and that she wasn't being swayed by Asta's arguments. But apparently she had been swayed, because the only thing Litney did was to stare at him, then shift her gaze to Asta's outstretched paw. When he still did nothing, Litney said, "Dokken, I know you don't remember last time, but there were times when I rushed off and didn't think things through and that wasn't always—"

"But things turned out okay, didn't they?" Dokken interrupted.

"Only if you think dying was okay," Litney reminded him. "I think Asta's right. While I believe the water in there could certainly be what Gunner wants, I also have a feeling that taking three hours to look around isn't going to hurt." She paused, hoping Dokken would concede and agree. When he didn't, she said simply, "Dokken."

"Fine," he said with a deep sigh. "Whatever," and he stalked away without shaking the bear's paw.

Litney watched him go. She turned to Current and said, "Where else do you think we should look?"

6

IT WAS ODD, WALKING AROUND the property when Talmoon and Pansy weren't there. It made Litney feel as if she were doing something wrong, like she was spying on Talmoon and Pansy. But that wasn't it at all. If she and the others didn't look around—at everything—how could they ever find out what it was they were looking for?

After deciding they didn't want to freak their parents out, Litney and Dokken made quick phone calls home to tell their parents everything was fine, but that their friends still needed help. Then Current led them around to all of the remaining outbuildings on the farm. Since most of them were empty, none elicited much interest, except for Pansy's gardening shed, which was only a little bigger than an outhouse. Inside there were what looked like bunches of dried weeds hanging from the ceiling and some old glass jars sitting on a shelf. "What are those?" Litney asked, pointing above her head.

"Pansy collects different plants from the wetlands and dries the leaves for teas and poultices," the dog informed her.

"Poultices?" Dokken asked. He had a weed dangling from his mouth. "You mean like chicken?"

Litney giggled as Current explained, "That's poultry. Poultices are mashed-up things like leaves or spices or moss that can be put on wounds or to help coughs."

"She makes tea from some of these?" Asta inquired of the dog who had stepped inside the building and was sniffing each and every corner.

"Yes," Current said when he looked up, and there was a little leaf stuck to the left side of his nose. "Why?"

"Because tea is a liquid," Asta pointed out.

"Who in the world would kidnap someone for tea?" Dokken snorted.

"Um, go a bit further back than stills and moonshine and you'll find tea was the thing governments controlled. You know," Litney prodded when Dokken still didn't seem to understand, "The Boston Tea Party?"

"Yeah, but that was over taxation," Dokken said, rolling his eyes.

"Yes, but tea was a huge thing. It's at least a possibility," Litney argued.

The boy rolled his eyes again. "Come on. Seriously? Look, we've considered everything out here, and nothing comes close to what we are after except what is in that barn. Don't you think we should go find Gunner and tell him about the water in there?"

"We haven't checked the house yet," Litney said, even though she, too, was now nearly certain that they could go to Gunner. She wasn't as annoyed as Dokken at the delay, but she felt that, as soon as they went through the house, they had been as thorough as they could be. She hoped Asta agreed. She didn't like it that Asta and Dokken seemed to be getting more and more at odds.

"Do we have to do the house?" Dokken moaned, bending down to tie a shoe that had come untied.

"Yes. Let's make sure."

Since Asta couldn't fit through the front door of the house, she told the others she would keep nosing around outside, just in case they had missed anything. "But let me know if anything catches your eye. And I mean anything. We have no idea what we're after, and we need to be open to anything and everything."

After promising her they would, the two kids followed Current inside. They all felt they had given the kitchen enough attention, so they went down the hall, opening closets, pulling books off the bookshelves that lined the hallway's walls.

"Nothing," Dokken said with a sigh, when what he really meant was, "I told you so."

"Follow Current," she said, pushing his back until they reached the first room off to their left. It must have been a guest room. It contained one bed and one empty dresser, and that was it.

The bathroom was next, and it didn't have anything unusual in it. The counter had two toothbrushes, an eyelash curler, and two bars of soap—one in the bathtub underneath a razor and one at the sink. They continued on and came to the bedroom that had to be Talmoon and Pansy's. It had no closet, but one wall sported a row of pegs from which their clothes hung, except for the one peg that held a bright yellow purse about the size of an envelope. The bed was shaped like a sleigh and had a thick, voluminous white comforter tossed on top of it. Talmoon had two pairs of boots in one corner, Pansy had three pairs of sandals and one pair of slippers in another. There was a dresser, but a quick embarrassed glance by Litney into the drawers showed only undergarments and nightgowns.

"Can we leave now?" Dokken demanded. "We've searched everywhere and found nothing. It's obvious that it's the water in the barn."

"We haven't searched everywhere," the dog said quietly.

As they stepped into what was obviously Talmoon's studio at the end of the house, Litney saw that this was where the roof gave out. There was no ceiling above them, only sky ruggedly framed by the erratic stoppings and startings of beams and shingles.

The ceiling wasn't the only thing with holes in it. When Litney looked down at the floor, she saw that the planks of wood didn't butt up one against the other. There was about a half an inch of space between them. Apparently there was no sub-floor beneath those planks either, because all over the studio, thorny bushes had shot up through the cracks. The shrubs sported leaves turning slightly brown around the edges since it was October. Dokken asked her what the plants were. She had been sent often enough out into the patch at her grandparents' farm to recognize those thistly canes. "Raspberries."

After thinking all those bushes made the studio appear forlorn and uncared for, Dokken turned to Current and asked, "Why would Talmoon allow them to grow up in here?"

The dog hesitated, almost as if he might be about to reveal a secret. Then he must have decided it was okay, because he replied, "Talmoon believes in the beauty and power of nature."

"O . . . kay . . ." Dokken said, and he could certainly see how that was true after looking at the teapots in the barn. "But come on. Holes in the ceiling? Bushes growing up through the floor? Don't they get in the way? Try and take over?"

The dog lapped water from a bowl near the wall. When he turned back, water dripped from his mouth. He licked his lips and said, "Talmoon trusts they're there for a reason."

"Yeah," said Dokken, laughing, "Because he has holes in his floor."

Current's white cheeks puffed out in annoyance. "They're his teachers."

"His teachers?" Dokken shook his head. "You've got to be joking."

The dog's ears dropped, and he suddenly looked hopeless. It was almost as if he believed it was important that Litney and Dokken understand Talmoon's studio in order to be able to find what Gunner was looking for.

"Okay, sorry," Dokken hurried to apologize when he saw the dog's face. "That was rude. But, to be honest, I really don't get it. Please explain to me how bushes coming up through the floor of a studio can be a teacher. I'm serious. I want to know," Dokken added when the dog continued to stare at him.

"You won't understand because you don't want to understand. You would rather mock Talmoon." Current was looking just a little fierce.

Dokken shook his head. "No. I'm serious. Tell me."

Clearly, Current did not want to. But he had his master and mistress to think about, and he'd do anything to save them. "In the winter, when these bushes are dead and empty, they remind Talmoon that life does not go on forever." The dog paused, obviously waiting to see if Dokken was going to come back with some sort of smart-alleck remark. When the boy simply nodded, Current continued. "When they have swelling buds in the spring, they remind Talmoon of all we are capable of."

"Let me guess," Litney joined in, excitedly. "When they have fruit on them in the summer, they show Talmoon we all have something to offer."

The dog gave one simple nod of his head, but before he could continue, Dokken said in a sincere voice, "And I'll bet it's the importance of being able to let go of what we've made that's the final lesson in the fall."

Current didn't say anything for a moment. Then he admitted, "Perhaps I underestimated the two of you."

"Talmoon sounds like an amazing man. I'm sure you love him," Litney said softly.

The dog nodded his head once more but remained silent.

"Do you think what we're looking for is in here?" Dokken asked. Neither he nor Litney had moved any further into the studio. They were still standing just inside the doorway. Even though there were plants growing up through the floor and hardly any ceiling above them, somehow the space still felt sacred, as if terrible eternal consequences would follow if they did something wrong.

"I honestly don't know. My master lives out here with Pansy. He makes his teapots. That's all I know. I can't imagine what everyone is after."

"Do you think it's okay if we look around in here some?" she asked. "We promise to be careful."

"I want you to do anything you must to save them," the dog replied. Then he commenced to applying his nose to the floor of the studio.

Dokken began his search with the pottery supplies—Talmoon's wheel, his stool, the clay that was stored in a low cabinet along the wall. Those were all things he expected to find, but when he came across some small baskets containing different kinds of dried berries and some hull-like things, he asked Current what they were for.

"Talmoon collects those and some minerals from the wetlands and uses them to create his inks and glazes."

Knowing now what he did about the potter, this shouldn't have surprised Dokken, but it did. He assumed the inks and glazes would come in jars from some industrial plant, not backyard plants and simple things like berries.

Litney decided to start searching by examining some teapots that had already been made and were sitting on a shelf, obviously waiting to be fired in the kiln. While they had the same shape as the others, these were lifeless, as if they were waiting for the breath of fire to inspire them to beauty.

She wandered over to a beautiful oak bookcase with glass doors. She flipped the little piece of wood that held the doors closed and slowly opened them. Though the glass panels were perfectly intact, she had the feeling this bookcase was old. Not like twenty years old. More like two hundred years old.

On the top shelf, she saw a book that said LEDGER on its spine. It was almost as long as a newspaper and as thick as the huge dictionary Litney's parents had in their office at home. She heaved the ledger off the shelf and carried it over to a small table. Opening it to the page that had been bookmarked, she saw that Talmoon had kept an accounting of his most recent expenses and incomes. The last date that had been entered was two weeks earlier when he had paid to ship a teapot to Germany. As she flipped backwards through the pages, she saw the years slip by. When she got all the way to the front of the ledger, she saw that the very first entry was dated July 9th, 1923.

She did a double take. Nineteen twenty-three? That was . . . almost ninety years ago. Even if Talmoon had started making pottery professionally when he was only twenty, that would mean he was somewhere around 106 years old! Litney was never very good at guessing the ages of adults, but she knew Talmoon wasn't anywhere near that old. While she first recalled his height and that odd birthmark on his neck when she thought about what he looked like, she also remembered his hair had been quite brown, not even gray, let alone white. She decided he looked like he was somewhere in his late thirties, a bit younger than her father.

So how could this ledger be so old? Perhaps Talmoon's father, or even his grandfather, had also been a potter, and this ledger had been started by one of them and was passed on from one generation to the next. That had to be it, but as she paged through it more slowly, she could find no change in handwriting, let alone any acknowledgment that the book had passed from one person to another. With care and a little grunt, she returned the ledger back into its place on the top shelf.

The middle shelf of the bookcase housed an odd menagerie of things. There was a skull with teeth so long that it had to have belonged to a beaver.

There was a rock sporting a fossil of a fish whose petrified bones would have fit almost perfectly into Litney's palm, a couple of snake skins, one nest with a bright red ribbon wound through it, and a tomahawk. The tomahawk had a flat round stone secured on the end of it, and the handle was wrapped in what looked like soft leather. Litney glanced over her shoulder and saw that Current was occupied with something in the far corner. She decided to take the chance and reach out and touch the handle. The leather was so soft under her touch it almost felt as if it was going to melt. She withdrew her hand and saw one feather dangled from near the top of the tomahawk while three others trailed off the bottom of it. She wanted to pick it up and feel its heft in her hand, but she didn't dare risk it.

With a sigh, she turned her attention to the bottom shelf, which was empty, save for one wooden box about the size of a toaster. She bent down, pulled the wooden box out and put it on the small table. Opening the box, she saw it housed three things. The first was a tiny silver spoon with the initials TWS engraved on the end. She guessed this was Talmoon's baby spoon, although she had a hard time imagining the huge man ever being small enough to use a spoon that size.

The second thing in the wooden box was a note written on thick, beautiful pale-lilac paper. This was obviously personal, and Litney hated to do this, but she didn't want to risk missing anything, so she opened it and read:

Talmoon, I am yours. Forever. Pansy

Except for the word forever being underlined, the message was as simple and unadorned as could be.

Even more sure now that it was the water in the fountains that everyone was after, Litney pulled out the final thing in the wooden box—a photograph. It was a picture of two men, standing side by side, and while it was a black-and-white photograph, it was unlike any other black-and-white photograph she had seen before. In all of those, the tones had been sharp and distinct, ranging only from white to gray to black. This photo she examined was a touch blurry and it was more brown and cream than black and white. As with the bookcase, she had a feeling this photograph with its worn edges was very old.

In the photograph, neither of the men smiled as they stared at the camera. One was dressed in buckskins and had two long black braids hanging against his chest. He was obviously a Native American and he held a pipe in one hand and a tomahawk in the other. Not a tomahawk, Litney realized with a start as she turned to look at the middle shelf, *the* tomahawk. The top feather had the same brown streak running down one side. Plus, the rock was the exact same shade and shape. The man holding it had a face that seemed strong and more than a little sad, and as she examined the picture more closely, Litney realized his head didn't even reach the second man's shoulder.

This second man, who was gigantic, held a teapot in his hands, and he looked exactly like Talmoon. What alarmed Litney even more was that there was an obvious birthmark on the man's neck. Not only was it right where Talmoon's birthmark had been, it was the exact same shape. But it couldn't be. That would be impossible. She needed Dokken to look and tell her she wasn't crazy.

"Dokken," Litney urged. "Come here."

"Did you find something?" he asked when he wandered over.

She shrugged as she handed Dokken the photograph. She waited for him to think the same thing she had, but when he gave her the picture back without so much as a word, she stared at him, open-mouthed.

"Yeah, so." It was his turn to shrug.

She walked over to the bookshelf and pointed to the tomahawk. She shook the picture in front of Dokken's face. "It's the exact same one."

He looked doubtful, so he snatched the picture from her hand, stared hard at it for a moment, then turned his attention to the real tomahawk sitting in front of him. He shrugged. "Could be. Again, so?"

This time she pointed at the tall man. "Who does that remind you of?"

"It's probably his great-great-grandfather or something. You saw how big Gunner was. I'm sure tallness runs in the family."

"And you don't see anything else that arouses your curiosity," she said.

Dokken glanced at the photo once more, obviously doing it to satisfy Litney and not because he expected to find anything. "No," he pronounced. "I don't see anything else that arouses my curiosity."

"Ugh!" she growled. "Look. There." She pointed at the birthmark on the man's neck.

"Huh, looks like Florida, doesn't it?" Dokken mused.

"Yes, and . . . ." she said, waiting for it to hit him.

"And what?" he demanded. "What's wrong with you?"

"What's wrong with you?" Litney exclaimed. "That's Talmoon. It has to be. Talmoon has that same birthmark on his neck. Right next to his Adam's apple. Just like this man. Didn't you notice it?"

"No. I was more concerned with his 'I could crush you' height than with some stupid thing on his neck," Dokken snapped.

"Talmoon has that same exact birthmark in the same exact place."

"Are you sure? How do you know it's in the same exact place?" Dokken insisted.

It took her a moment to answer. "Because when Pansy stood on her tiptoes to kiss his shoulder, I saw it there. And," she paused, using her memory and her hands, "and Pansy stood on this side of him, which would have been his right side, and she kissed that shoulder, which would have been his right shoulder. See?" she said, referring to the picture once again. "It's on his right side."

"That doesn't mean anything. I have a mole on my chest that all the Carver men have. It's the same size, shape and in the same place as my dad's and granddad's. Beside this photograph had to have been taken over a hundred years ago. Maybe even a hundred and fifty. It isn't possible."

"The ledger!" Litney exclaimed, dashing to the bookshelf. "Here, look at this." She flipped to the bookmarked page and showed him the most recent entry. "Now, look." She went back through the pages all the way to the beginning and showed him the date of 1923.

"Again, that could have been his father's or grandfather's book," he argued, thinking she had lost it this time.

"Not if you look closely at the handwriting. See?" she said, pointing to the most recent entry and then comparing that to the first entry in the book. "It's the same. The exact same."

"I don't know," he retorted, eyeing the book closely.

With one finger, she pointed at the "p" in teapot on the most recent entry. "Notice how whoever wrote this brought the pencil to the right with a little flick on the stem of the p?" She heaved the pages until she was at the front of the book again. "It's the same here. The handwriting is the same all through the ledger."

Dokken narrowed his eyes. "Let me get this straight. You're saying this guy in the picture is Talmoon? That Talmoon has been making pots for eight or nine decades? He's old, but he's not *that* old. You know what," he said, snapping his fingers. "I'll bet this is one of those old-time photo thingies. When my parents took me to Niagara Falls when I was six, we went into one of those. We had a hard time deciding between Old West or Gangster, but we finally chose a Saloon, and I got to wear one of those big ten-gallon hats and chaps. I even got to strap on a holster. When they handed us the picture after it was developed, it really looked real. And old. That would explain this."

Litney's lips pursed as she stared at the picture again. He could be right. She had seen those kinds of photos before in some of her friends' houses, and they did look real. But something told her that wasn't the case here. This picture didn't just look old, it *was* old. If that were the case . . . "What if—" Litney began, then stopped herself. It couldn't be true. That couldn't be what everyone was after, because it was only a myth. It wasn't real. It couldn't be.

7

"It's obvious," Dokken said in answer to Asta's question as to what they should do next. "We figure out how to find Gunner, tell him we've found what he's looking for, and then we go home. It's lasagna night tonight, and I don't want to miss it." Dokken's voice was raised so Asta, outside, could hear him. He and Litney sat in the kitchen with Current.

Litney got up from her place at the table and turned the burner off on the stove when the tea kettle whistled. As Dokken and Asta had argued about what they should do, Litney had decided she wanted some tea. She had asked Current where Pansy kept the teabags, filled the kettle with water from the pump outside and started the water to boil. "Oh," she said to Current because it had just occurred to her. "I know this is a silly question to ask, but is there a teapot around here I can use to steep the tea in?"

Current lifted his nose to a small shelf over the sink. "That's the one Pansy always uses."

She carefully took it down from its place and set it on the countertop, studying it for a moment. "Is this one of Talmoon's? It looks different than the ones I saw in the barn."

The dog cocked his head. "To be honest, I don't know. I know it's the one Pansy's used for as long as I can remember, but I've never heard if Talmoon made it or not."

Examining it more closely, she decided it had a shape similar to Talmoon's pots, but it wasn't quite the same. This one was taller and less exact. One side of the pot was round while another side was almost flat. While this could have been because the potter who made it wasn't very good, Litney didn't think that was the case. It felt intentional, almost as if the potter knew nothing was perfect and wanted to make a pot that reflected that.

The glaze on the pot was also startlingly different. The other pots she had seen in the barn tended to be in light blues, creams, browns, or grays. She guessed this was because then Talmoon had a canvas on which he could do his brushstrokes. This pot in her hands now, however, was not only black, but there was a blueness to it that was so strong it shone. Eventually she shrugged, because it didn't really matter one way or the other if Talmoon had made it or not. Turning to face everyone else, she asked, "Does anyone else want some tea?"

"No," Dokken said with a shudder. "Tea tastes like dirty water to me."

Current shooks his head while Asta replied from the doorway, "No, thank *you*."

Dokken sniped under his breath, "Are *you* sure *you* don't want some, Asta? Perhaps it's the magic liquid."

"Boy," the bear replied in a voice Litney had never heard before, "why don't *you* come out here and say that to my face?"

Dokken and Asta locked eyes for a moment in silent combat, then Dokken became very interested in a hangnail on his index finger.

Bothered as she was by this tension, Litney felt powerless. She didn't know what she could do or say to help get rid of it, so she sighed and returned her attention to the pot, dropping the tea bags into it. She had thought it would be great to have Asta here to help them, but if that little exchange were any indication, things between Dokken and Asta were getting worse. Much worse.

Litney felt torn between the two of them. What was she supposed to do? Whose opinion was she supposed to follow? Truth be told, she agreed with both of them. She wanted the water in the barn to be the answer so they could save Talmoon and Pansy and get them back home safe and sound as quickly as they could. She also thought Asta was right that they didn't want to rush and do something rash, because then they might miss the real thing they were after. What made everything worse was no matter what Dokken said, or how he scoffed at her, she was sure the photograph and the ledger meant something. And Asta had agreed with her—so much so that she had asked Litney to go back into Talmoon's studio to retrieve them. Litney had sat down on the front step and carefully opened the ledger. "See?" she had said to the bear. "It's the same handwriting in the beginning and at the end." And then she had shown Asta the picture, told her about the tomahawk and the birthmark. Litney had waited for Asta to proclaim her opinion about what it all meant, but the bear had only sat on her haunches and stayed mostly silent ever since.

Litney's stomach was beginning to roil and churn from all of this—it's what happened whenever she got upset. If only she knew what to do. She wanted to talk about it, but what should she say? She was sure to hurt someone's feelings, and she couldn't stand it when she did that.

She figured the tea had seeped enough, so she found a mug and poured the tea into it. When she sat down at the table, she sat as far away from Dokken as the table would allow. He was staring morosely out the door at Asta's back, and Litney was not in the mood to hear him continue complaining about how they were wasting time and how much he wanted to get back home.

Blowing on the tea a little to cool it, Litney took a sip. The tea tasted like flowers, popcorn, a splash of mint, all finished off by a dash of summer night. As Litney went back into her memory, she didn't think there was anything she had ever had to drink that could compare. It was delicious, soothing.

When she lowered the mug to the table, she wrapped her hands around its warmth. Since it was early fall, it felt good to draw the heat into her fingers. Litney continued to sip the tea, and as she did, the sharpness in her stomach began to dissipate. When she had emptied her mug, she refilled it and drank some more. Before long, she felt this liquid glow reaching to every part of her body. The only other time she had felt like this was after she had climbed out of the milkweed pod in the hiding tree on the first adventure—she remembered feeling strong, sure, ready to face what was ahead. How everything that had worried or upset her had faded away. It was the same now. When she happened to glance at her wrist, she saw the bracelet was glowing, almost as if it had been turned on like a lamp.

"Okay," Litney announced, standing up with not a trace of apology or apprehension. Dokken and Current turned to look at her while Asta put her head through the doorway. "This is annoying the candy canes out of me. Dokken, if you want to go home, go. I'll take care of this. But if you choose to stay, then we are not going to rush this. So quit crabbing and staring daggers at Asta. And Asta, I remember from last time that you like to be absolutely certain about things. We don't know what we are looking for, so unless some liquid stands up and starts shouting, 'Here I am! I'm what you want!,' we have to make a choice and go from there. It might be right, it might be wrong, but we still have to do something."

Had she just started speaking French with a perfect Parisian accent, Current, Asta and Dokken couldn't have stared harder at Litney. And not only was the bracelet glowing, but Dokken thought her face was, too. She had always been pretty, he guessed, but now, she was attractive in the sense that no one could tear their eyes away from her.

"What?" she demanded. "What are you all staring at? I was just sick of the tension, that's all." When the other three continued looking at her agape, she began to rub around her mouth. "Do I have something on my lips? Oh, no, there's nothing hanging from my nose, is there?"

"Litney," Dokken whispered. "You're beautiful."

Dokken's words hung in the air. "That's not what I meant. You're not beautiful," he backpedaled, standing up quickly from the table and knocking the bench over with a crash. He scrambled to right the bench, and it was then he realized what he had just said. "No, I mean you are, but you're not. Not that way." Then he headed for the door. He would have run straight into Asta in his attempt to flee if the bear hadn't moved out of the way.

"Give him some time," Asta counseled the girl when Litney began to dash after the retreating red-headed figure. When she struggled against Asta's paw that had come up to restrain her, Asta explained, "Time might help his embarrassment cool a little. He deserves that from you."

Litney watched Dokken escape into the barn, then went back to the table and sat down with a huff. She propped her elbow on the table and plopped her chin in her hand. "What was that about? And why were you all staring at me?" she demanded. "I only wanted you all to get along. I was tired of the tension."

"It was your face," Asta said simply.

"And the way you were talking," Current added. "It was like you were a president."

"Or a prophet," the bear said with a nod.

"What do you mean like a president or a prophet?" Litney asked, scrunching up her face in disbelief. "I wasn't talking about politics or God or anything."

"No, but you were speaking as if there was some strong power in you," Asta responded.

"That's ridiculous," Litney argued.

"No, it's not," Current told her. "It's true. Plus, your face had this weird light about it. Like you had eaten a spoonful of fireflies. That's what the boy meant."

"You can't be serious," she replied, still not buying it.

"Litney, have I ever lied to you or even exaggerated?" Asta asked.

She ran through all of her encounters with the bear, then said, "No, you haven't."

"So believe me when I tell you something happened to you. Something . . . shone through you. You couldn't feel it?" Asta inquired.

Litney could recall with ease how upset her stomach had been before drinking the tea. Then by the time she had finished the first mug, she had already felt strong and sure. "What in the world could have happened?" she asked, a slight tremble in her voice.

"It happened as you were sitting at the kitchen table," Current observed.

"What? You think it could have been the tea?" She opened the lid to the teapot and pulled out the tea bags. Most tea bags that she had seen before were made out of a kind of paper that had been stapled shut; then a string led from the bag to a little tag of paper These almost seemed to be made out of a dull white fabric, and, instead of being stabled shut, they were tied shut with the string. "Did Pansy make these?"

"Yes," Current answered. "She uses cheesecloth to make the bags and then ties them off herself."

"How in the world would you know it's cheesecloth?" Litney asked.

"Pansy likes an audience when she's cooking. She'll make me sit right here, and then she'll pretend like she's teaching me how to cook."

"Like a cooking show on television?" Litney asked.

"I don't know what you mean," the dog replied.

"Television. A . . . box that has people on it," she told the dog.

"A box with people on it? You mean they're standing on top of it?"

"No," she laughed. "I mean they are *in* it."

"In the box? Are they trapped? Like a cage?"

"No," she laughed again, exasperated, wondering how far back she had to go to explain this. "Something called a camera takes pictures of people." Litney glanced around the kitchen and found a small frame propped up beside the sink. She dropped the tea bags she had been holding back into the tea pot, went over to the small frame, and saw it held a picture of a girl standing on some steps, wearing white gloves. She remembered how Pansy had told them she went over to her grandmother's in the afternoons for tea. Pointing at it, she said, "I'll bet this is a picture of Pansy, taken when she was young. Pictures capture an image. Well, with television, the camera can capture not only one picture, it can capture a series of images, and the images move and talk and dance and fly. And then other people, like myself, sit in front of the television—the box—and watch the moving pictures. It's entertaining. And one kind of program a person can watch is a cooking show. Just like Pansy, the person prepares food and tells the audience how to do it."

Current lifted his nose in the air. "I wouldn't let a box teach me how to cook."

"Oh, but it's fun. You end up trying all sorts of things you might never have tried, might never have even imagined."

"Litney, if you are done expounding on the delights of television, could you please bring one of the tea bags over here?"

Litney plucked one out of the tea pot and carried it over to the door where Asta's nose gave it a big wet sniff. "Do you know what's in here?" she asked Current.

"Those things we saw in the shed. Things from the wetlands."

"How did this make you feel?" Asta asked Litney.

"Strong. Sure. Magical," Litney added the last word somewhat unwillingly. It felt over-the-top, but it was undeniable.

"Does Pansy know magic?" Asta inquired of Current. "Could she have put a spell on the tea to make it so powerful?"

"I don't know," the dog answered, shaking his head. "I really don't."

Asta smelled the tea bags once again. "While nothing smells out of the ordinary, perhaps we have our answer," she ventured at last.

"You think it's the tea everyone's after?" Litney clarified.

"There's no denying it transformed you," Asta answered. Then she added, "For a while. Look," Asta said to Current. "It's fading."

"Indeed," Current said, looking at the girl's face that was now back to normal. "And the bracelet is quiet again," he added, lifting his nose toward her wrist.

When she looked down and saw the bracelet did not shine anymore, Litney was sure they had their answer.

THE THREE OF THEM AGREED IT would be best (in other words, less embarrassing) if Current went to retrieve Dokken. The dog stepped into the barn and took so long to return that Litney asked Asta, "What if he doesn't come out?"

"He'll come out. See?" she lowered her voice to a whisper as the boy followed Current out of the barn.

Asta didn't want to allow any time for things to feel awkward, so immediately, she said, "It appears we have two choices before us—either the liquid everyone is after is the water from the barn or it's the tea made from Pansy's tea bags. Both of them are certainly possibilities, but Dokken, of those two, which do you think is more likely?"

Dokken hadn't looked up ever since he stepped out of the barn, and when he did now, he gazed at Asta with eyes that questioned the bear's sincerity. He seemed to be saying, "Yeah, sure, like you really want my opinion." However, Asta's face indicated that she had asked the question because she really wanted to know what the boy's feelings on the matter were. "I sat in there a long time," Dokken began in answer. "I even tasted the water a bunch of different times, from all of the different waterfalls, in fact. The water tasted delicious, but it didn't do anything to me." Dokken's voice had gotten quieter and quieter as he spoke, and now he finished in almost a whisper, "Nothing like what the tea did to Litney."

"You think it's the tea?" Litney asked.

Dokken didn't meet her eyes when he answered, "It has to be the tea. Is that what you all think?"

"Yes," Current and Litney replied without hesitation.

"How about you, Asta? What do you think?" Dokken asked. He was smart enough to know that all of them were waiting to hear Asat's pronouncement, himself included.

"Yes, I think it's the tea," the bear said after a pause. "But the question is what do we do now? How do we get Gunner back here?"

All of them were at a loss. Gunner hadn't told them how they could contact him. He had simply said three days was all they had. Now that they knew what the magical liquid was, they couldn't help but feel hugely frustrated by the situation. If only they could get Gunner back, they could save Talmoon and Pansy.

It was Current who surprised them with his idea. "Why don't you use that?" he asked, pointing his nose at Litney's bracelet. "You said it had all sorts of powers."

The suggestion was so obvious, Litney couldn't believe she hadn't thought of it. What wasn't as obvious was how she could use the bracelet to get Gunner here. She stared at the bracelet for a bit, then decided she would try talking into it—like it was some sort of wristwatch walkie talkie. She pulled her wrist up to her mouth, cleared her throat, and said, "Gunner? We have found what you're after. Please come and tell us what you want us to do with it."

Dokken looked dubious. "That sounded like something you'd hear at the grocery store. 'Clean up in Aisle Seven.' You really think that's going to get him here?" he said. "Besides, wouldn't that work only if he had a bracelet to receive the message?"

In the past, Litney would have doubted herself. She would have said, "Yeah, sorry. What do you think I should have done?" But not this time. Litney knew this was going to work. She was certain.

⁕ 8 ⁕

THREE HOURS LATER, LITNEY WASN'T so certain that talking into the bracelet had been the way to get Gunner to return. "Got any other bright ideas?" Dokken asked smarmily, first looking at Current, then Litney.

"We could jump down the well and go to Gad ourselves," Litney suggested as she carefully finished wrapping as many tea bags as she could find in a dish towel. There had been six tea bags in the kitchen, but she had a feeling there had to be more somewhere. When she had gone outside to the garden shed, she had found that one of the glass jars on the shelf contained at least thirty more. Wanting to make sure she was bringing the right stuff, she made sure to smell each and every one before she put it in the dish towel—luckily they all smelled the same.

When the tea bags were secure, she stared down at them, worried the king might demand more. She could only hope she had found enough to satisfy him, and that's when it occurred to her that she could hand over these tea bags and the king still might not let Talmoon and Pansy go. Wasn't that what often happened in the movies and all those Nancy Drew novels she used to love to read? She decided she couldn't worry about that, because she didn't know what else to do. She figured if the king doubled-crossed her, she'd have to deal with that when it happened. Maybe she'd use the bracelet and see if she could turn him into a newt. She smiled at that as she picked up the towel holding the tea bags and walked out the door. Dokken and Current followed.

"I don't think you want to jump down the well," Asta said in the same way her mother would have as the four of them wandered toward the barn. About every fifteen minutes or so, they would head in that direction to look out over the wetlands and see if they could spot Gunner.

"No, I don't want to jump down the well," Litney replied as evenly as she could manage, "but I will if that's the only way I can save Pansy and Talmoon."

Current, who had dashed ahead to the edge of the yard, barked once. It was such a normal dog sound that it startled the humans. They hurried over to the dog as he barked again. Both his body and ears lowered as he growled, "He's here."

Litney and Dokken peered out into the wetlands, and sure enough, there was Gunner walking toward the farm. It didn't take long for Litney to figure out what Gunner was carrying over one shoulder—his shotgun. "Asta, maybe you'd better hi—," she began, turning around to talk to the bear, but Asta was gone. She could only hope Asta would find someplace to hide where Gunner wouldn't look.

"So you think you've found it," Gunner shouted when he got close enough that they could hear him. He sounded as if his favorite team had just won a championship.

Neither Litney nor Doken responded.

"Well?" he barked, when he came to stand right in front of them. His whole body seemed to hum from impatience. "Did you find it or not?"

"We think so," Litney replied.

"You'd better do more than *think*, missy. You called me out here, so you better be sure," Gunner growled and repeated. "Did you find it or not?"

"Sir, we think it's the tea made from Pansy's tea bags. Litney had some this morning, and she was, well . . ." Dokken paused and felt his face burst hot with embarressment. He was sure it had turned as red as an apple, but he soldiered on, "Well, she was transformed."

"Do you have any more of this tea?" the big man demanded.

Litney pulled open the yellow purse she had borrowed from Pansy's bedroom. Gently pulling out the towel, she opened it up and held up one of the tea bags.

"No, I mean actual tea," Gunner said, clenching his jaw.

"Just a minute." Litney carefully put the towel back in the purse, and then dashed back into the house to grab the mug she had prepared, thinking Gunner might want proof She had added two more bags to the pot and made sure to brew it nice and strong. The tea had cooled hours ago, but she hoped that didn't matter. Walking carefully back across the yard, she offered Gunner the mug. He put his gun on the ground and downed the tea in one swallow. Litney saw a terrible glee light the man's eyes, but before he said anything aloud, he reached into his pocket and withdrew the little green bottle he had drunk out of when Litney and Dokken had first met him. He took a swig of this, and after wiping his mouth with the back of his hand, Gunner leaned back and gave a whoop followed by a holler. "Well, kick me in the behind and give me a Sunday washing. You did it. You two did it!" he exclaimed. He took a couple of deep breaths, and then he said, "All right, then. We'd better get to the well so you two can head back to Gad and save my dear brother."

"You don't care about your brother," Dokken said pointedly.

"What did you say, boy?" Gunner's good mood was gone in an instant as his forehead turned into a thunderhead—gathering and dangerous. "I've already told you once, you really need to learn to control that mouth of yours."

"Dokken," Litney impolred when she could see Dokken was going to say something more. She rested a hand on his shoulder.

The boy shrugged off her hand and said, "It's true. We may be only kids, but it doesn't take an adult to figure out that you betrayed your brother. I don't know how you met up with those Gadlandians, or whatever you call them, or why you would sell out your brother, but it's obvious you did. Why would you do such a thing? What's in it for you? Do you know what kind of place they have him in?" Dokken knew he was shouting now and probably soon dead meat, but he was not finished. "And Pansy, for goodness sake. They are probably doing the same thing to her!"

"No!" Gunner shouted, marching over to Dokken. The big man grabbed the boy's t-shirt and hauled him up close to his face. "They swore they wouldn't do anything to Pansy. Only to Talmoon. Now I suggest," here the man took a couple of deep breaths, and the red in his face started to recede a little, "you all get yourself down that well and give the king the tea bags. Then get Talmoon and Pansy back here. You get what I'm saying?" He let go of Dokken so abruptly, the boy stumbled backwards and fell into the dirt.

"Yeah, I've got it," he muttered, standing up and dusting off his hands. "Believe me, I got it."

"Good. Now get up on that well and jump," the man commanded.

"Can't I get some gloves first?" Litney asked. She remembered how cold her fingers had gotten on the previous trips through the well.

"I don't care about your stupid little fingers. Just that you have those tea bags safe and secure. Let me see how you're carrying them again," Gunner said.

"But you just saw how I was carrying them," she replied.

"Show me."

How was it Gunner and Talmoon could say so little and scare her so much? Litney tugged on a string around her neck. She pulled out the yellow purse she had tucked safely inside her shirt. Opening the flap of the purse, she unwrapped the small kitchen towel nestled inside. "See?" she pointed to the tea bags. "Safe."

"Fine. Now put that back inside your shirt to keep it extra safe. Good. Okay, both of you climb up there. That's it. Get those to the king as quickly as you can and get Pansy out of there," Gunner commanded.

"What about your dear old brother? Don't you want us to save him?" Dokken asked under his breath. Before the man could yell at him, Dokken gave a little wave, then jumped down the well.

Litney shrugged, then followed.

"We were getting worried," the king murmured when the two of them came to stand before him. As soon as they had returned to Gad, the alarm had sounded again. Not surprisingly (and none too gently), they had been immediately apprehended and carried to the king.

As they stood before him now, Litney saw that the king, whose fur was reddish orange, sat on a large silver throne in the middle of a dais made of ornately carved wood. The king wore a pelt of soft white fur around his shoulders, and his neck feathers—which rested on top of the pelt—had been decorated with gold beads and jewels. He was powerfully built and beautiful, that was until one looked in his eyes. His eyes were like an alleyway at night—vacant, dark and scary. Litney felt as if she would lose something important if she allowed herself to look into his eyes for very long. She stood a little taller, steeling herself to stay brave and strong. Thank goodness Dokken was standing beside her.

The king continued. "We thought we were going to have to do some real . . . inviting of Talmoon to tell us where to find what we were after. We could hardly imagine what was so important that you would dare neglect the welfare of your friends for so long."

Litney knew the king was trying to make her feel guilty, unsettled. Why else would he have stood up and started pacing like that, as if he were on the prowl and about to attack? Some instinct inside her told her she should not show any fear. She was relieved when her voice was steady as she replied, "We're here now. What do you want?"

Without warning, the king coiled his powerful legs and leapt through the air, landing directly in front of them. Dokken jumped while Litney let out a little scream. So much for not showing fear. "You know what I want," the king's bird-like face hissed, just inches from her own. "I will have it now."

"F-first you need to bring us Talmoon and Pansy," Dokken stuttered when he saw that Litney appeared momentarily immobile.

"F-first you need to learn to keep your mouth shut," the king parroted cruelly, turning his attention to Dokken and staring the boy down. When Dokken looked away, the king laughed. "How in the world can you imagine you have any power in this situation?" Strolling back to his throne and sitting down with a flourish, the king continued to stare at Dokken. "I'm serious. I want to know how you can think you have any power? What is it with you,

you humans? You think you can be in control of everything. Make demands. Get your way. Take Gunner for instance. He was quite insistent that the dear woman . . . what's her name?" the king turned to Miss Bootlicker who was standing beside him.

Miss Bootlicker, who had been watching impassively, answered, "Pansy."

"Ah, yes. Pansy. That's a flower, isn't it? In your world? Her name fits her. She is beautiful, no?"

The kids nodded, because the king seemed to expect an answer.

Leaning forward, the king said, "She will not be beautiful for long if you do not hand over what I'm after."

"How do we know you haven't already hurt her?" Litney said slowly, making sure not to stutter or hesitate.

"You don't."

"But—"

"Hand . . . it . . . over. Miss Bootlicker, if you would, please."

As Miss Bootlicker approached, Litney flashed a look at Dokken. What should she do? Dokken raised his eyebrows and shook his head. He had no idea.

For a brief second, Litney thought about using the bracelet, but then she saw the two guards standing on either side of the dais, and four more behind her by the door. All of them were holding the same needle-looking things that the guards outside of Talmoon's cell had been holding. The weird blue liquid and the thick sharp needles were quite convincing that she needed to be far more certain about how to use the bracelet before attempting something in a situation like this. Plus, if something did go wrong, the king could discover the power of the bracelet, and she certainly didn't want that. Litney decided she would hand over the tea bags and hope the king would be true to his word and let Talmoon and Pansy go.

Tugging at the string around her neck, Litney pulled the yellow purse out from its safe hiding place inside her shirt. "Here," she said as she pulled out the towel that held the tea bags and offered it to Miss Bootlicker.

"A towel?" the creature sounded bewildered. "But I thought—"

"Unwrap it," Litney told her. "Those are tea bags in there. You need to put them in boiling water to make the liquid."

Miss Bootlicker turned and looked at the king, who bellowed at her, "Well, don't just stand there. Get boiling water."

She hurried from the room, leaving through a door behind the throne. As they stood in the silence that followed her departure, Litney started to shift from foot to foot. She wanted to tell the king that he had what he wanted and so he needed to release Talmoon and Pansy right now, but it didn't take a rocket scientist to figure out what the king's answer would be—he would say he needed to make sure the tea bags worked. Litney's stomach lurched at this. What if the tea bags didn't work? What if they weren't the magical thing everyone wanted? What would happen to her and Dokken? To Pansy and Talmoon? When Litney glanced at Dokken, it appeared he was as worried as she was. He lifted a hand to drag it through his hair and she could see that it was shaking.

It was taking Miss Bootlicker so long to return that Litney wondered if she had needed to start a fire to boil the water. After all, she remembered that tepid water Miss Bootlicker had served as "tea" the first time they had met her. Maybe they didn't have anything that could get something to boiling, or even hot enough for the tea to steep.

She had her answer forty-five minutes later when Miss Bootlicker finally returned, carrying what looked like a witch's cauldron. It was so huge, Litney had no idea how the creature could lift it. Setting it down on the floor with a clang, Miss Bootlicker pointed to the steam that was drifting out of the pot. With what sounded like a mixture of embarrassment and frustration, Miss Bootlicker muttered, "It was boiling, but it isn't now. Will it still work?"

"Yes," Litney replied, stepping forward. "I guess I was wrong to say it had to be boiling. It needed to be just really warm."

"That would have been helpful to know," Miss Bootlicker muttered.

Litney, who hadn't heard what Miss Bootlicker had said, continued, "And in fact, we don't need this much water. That is, unless you want to use every single tea bag right now."

"No!" the king shouted as if she had just suggested she spend every last bit of money he owned. "We will use just one. One. One!"

"Okay," Litney said, looking at Dokken out of the corners of her eyes. There was no doubt in Litney's mind that the king was unstable. Trying not to draw too much attention to himself, Dokken lifted a finger to his temple and spun it around as if he was agreeing with her and saying, "Yeah, cuckoo."

"Do you have a small cup we can use?" Litney directed her question to Miss Bootlicker whose neck feathers were all akimbo. The creature took a deep breath and the feathers seemed to settle back into place. "Yes, I can find you a cup you can use."

This time, Miss Bootlicker returned quickly, and there was no need to sit against a wall and wait like Litney and Dokken had the last time the creature had left the room. Handing the cup to Litney, she asked, "Will this work?"

"That will be fine," Litney's hand shook slightly as she took the cup. She hoped it would be fine. She hoped it would work. Carefully, Litney scooped some of the hot water out of the pot and dropped one tea bag in. The king, who had been lounging kittywampus in the throne and singing a horrible song about humans' heads popping like balloons, sat up straight and stared hard at her. "What do we do with it?" he inquired.

"You drink it," she said as she started to pull the tea bag out.

"I will not!" he cried, leaping up out of the throne and knocking the cup out of her hand. It flew across the room and shattered when it hit the floor. "You are trying to poison me!" The king grabbed her by the neck and started to lift her up off the floor.

"My lord," Miss Bootlicker hissed in his ear. "Put the girl down."

"I will not. She is trying to kill me. She is trying to ruin it all!"

Litney wanted to breathe. She wanted to be walking through a forest on a beautiful summer day and pull in gobfulls of lovely pure oxygen that all the nice trees had made for her. When she couldn't, she saw the edges of her world begin to darken.

Dokken intended to jump on the king to make him let Pansy go, but several guards managed to get the massive needles only inches away from his stomach before he could even make a move. He held still.

"My lord!" Miss Bootlicker repeated, more insistent. "Put her down. I'll drink the tea for *you*. I'll be the one who makes sure it works."

"You will?" the king sounded like a child pleading with his mother to make everything okay.

"I will. Now put her down. There. Good. Thank *you*."

Litney didn't crumple to the floor, but that was only because Miss Bootlicker was holding her up under the arms. "You'll be okay," she whispered. More loudly, she addressed the rest of the room in her formal voice, "Let's try this again, shall we?" With that, the creature propped Litney up on her feet and left by the door behind the throne.

Litney managed to stay on her feet, but she was having a hard time thinking—the cloud that had descended on her when the king had been squeezing her throat would not clear. As she rubbed her neck and took some deep breaths, her mind was able to flit to the fact that Miss Bootlicker had sounded so kind. But why? The creature had never been anything but distant, creepy and threatening before. She didn't feel any better when her mind started to clear, because now there was nothing to stop fear from crashing through her. She was terrified that neither she and Dokken, nor Talmoon and Pansy were ever going to make it out of there.

When Miss Bootlicker returned with another cup, Litney hoarsely said, "Thank *you*," and dipped it into the hot water. After she dropped the tea bag into the cup, she told the king, who was pacing back and forth in front of her, "It won't be long now." She let the tea steep longer than she needed to, but that was only because she was afraid that it wasn't going to work. Finally, when she could put it off no longer, she removed the bag from the cup and offered it to Miss Bootlicker. "Here."

The cup looked ludicrous in the creature's oversize hands, but slowly and carefully, she raised it to her lips and took a small drink. "How much do I need to drink?" she inquired after a few more sips.

"It should kick in pretty soon," Litney said, hoping. Since nothing seemed to be happening yet, she urged, "Drink more if you can, though."

Soon, the cup was empty—Miss Bootlicker stared at the bottom of the cup, Litney stared at Miss Bootlicker, and the king stared at Litney. When several minutes had passed, Litney asked, "Do you feel anything yet?"

Miss Bootlicker inhaled deeply and said, "I feel a bit more relaxed than I did awhile ago." Her eyes found the king's to see if that was an acceptable answer.

Obviously it wasn't, because the king leapt once again to Litney's side, this time grabbing her fiercely by the arm. "What are you playing at, little girl?" he growled as he shook her. Punctuating every consonant, he ground out, "This . . . is . . . not . . . it! What did you think you were going to do? Give us the wrong stuff and come out of this alive?"

It hadn't worked, Litney thought frantically as the king glared at her. But it had worked back at the farm. How could they have been wrong? Talmoon . . . Pansy . . . what was going to happen now? "I-I-I—."

The king cut her off. "You-you-you and your friend are going to pay. Guards!"

All the guards in the room began to close in with their huge needles pointed and ready.

"Wait!" Miss Bootlicker shouted, stepping between Litney and Dokken and the guards. Litney was sure now that Miss Bootlicker was kind. She was going to save them. However, Miss Bootlicker's next words proved Litney dead wrong. "Are you . . . are you really going to let them off that easy? By just killing them?"

Litney felt her mouth fall open. Miss Bootlicker was urging the king to torture her and Dokken. Dokken's normally pale face blanched even further so that his freckles stood out like red cardinals on a snowy field.

"What are you suggesting?" the king ground out from between his clenched teeth, still squeezing Litney's arm.

"Throw them under into the Darkness That Never Ends. See how they like trying to stay away from the Breath Bandits."

The king still seemed to be wavering, so Miss Bootlicker added, "And don't forget the Ignitatus."

Litney swore she saw and felt the king shudder. He dropped her arm and stepped away from her, returning to the throne. "Hmmm," he said, fixing the mantle around his neck that had gone askew. "I think you might be right. Death is too kind, too quick for traitors such as these. I'm all for some good-old fashioned terror. As ever, Miss Bootlicker, I am grateful for your counsel. Guards! Take them to the Door and throw them in. Make sure you lock it behind them." The king paused and then narrowed his eyes. "Feel free to stick around and listen for their screams."

* 9 *

THE DARKNESS THAT HAD disconcerted Dokken at his new house was nothing compared to the complete blackness that engulfed him and Litney as soon as the guards closed the Door.

"Dokken?" Litney whispered.

He could feel her huddled up against his right side. "Yeah?" he answered, wishing his voice sounded braver, stronger, wishing he still had one of the flashlights they had used to follow Current through the night.

"I can't see anything."

This time, her whisper was so quiet, he could hardly hear her. "I know. Neither can I." He reached his hand back toward the Door, knowing it was foolish to hope he would find a handle. Still, he had to try. His hand met only a slick cold surface that was so flat, he couldn't even feel the edges of the door they had just been shoved through by the guards.

"What are we going to do?" Litney asked, then screamed. Dokken could no longer feel her beside him. Where had she gone? The only thing worse than being stuck down here in the dark was the thought of having to do it alone. Panicked, he reached out to feel for her when suddenly he felt himself slipping. He tumbled onto his back, and his body slid down, down, down.

"Ouch!" Litney exclaimed. "You landed on me."

"Gee, sorry," he replied sarcastically. "Next time I can't see a thing, I'll make sure to avoid landing on you."

After they had extricated themselves, she repeated, "I can't see a thing. Eyes open, eyes closed, it doesn't make any difference at all." Her breaths were coming in such quick short gasps, it sounded as if she had just gotten done sprinting.

"I know." He also knew that back in the throne room there had been mention of breath monsters and something else that sounded terrifying—ignitation or something, which sounded an awful lot like ignite or being set on fire.

"What are we going to do? I mean, really. Should we sit here? Should we stand up? It's not like we can walk anywhere. What if there's a hole? A canyon? A stray vat of boiling ooze? But if we sit here, what if there is something that can see us, but we can't see it? What if it starts to hunt us just like a cat with a mouse? What if it is closing in on us right now?"

While Dokken was as scared as he had ever been, the babble shooting out of Litney's mouth was coming so fast and furious that he had to laugh. When she heard his laughter, she tore into him. "Oh, *you* think this is funny. This is funny? How can this be funny?"

"It isn't funny," he tried to say in a serious voice.

"I can hear in *your* voice that *you* think this is hilarious. Didn't *you* hear what they said up there? About the Breath Bandits and the Ignitatus?"

"Yes, I heard, but we don't know what they are," he pointed out.

Litney huffed in exasperation. "And *you* think Breath Bandit sounds like a *good* thing? And an Ignitatus? What is that?"

"It sounds like it has something to do with fire," he offered.

"Exactly! I don't see any hot dogs or marshmallows lying around, so that doesn't sound particularly good to me," she said. "So what are we going to do?"

"Let's stand up, and—"

Litney interrupted him. "No. I think we should stay on our hands and knees. We're more stable that way."

"Well, don't ask me what I think we should do if *you* already know what *you* think we should do," Dokken grumbled.

"I didn't know what to do until *you* suggested something. You just happened to suggest the wrong thing." When this was met with silence, she said, "Dokken?" When he didn't answer again, she urged, "Say something."

"Okay. You annoy me."

"That's not very nice!"

"You told me to say something. I did."

"You have no idea how badly I want to tell you to get lost," Litney muttered.

"It's mutual, you know," Dokken replied.

When it occurred to Litney that Dokken could leave and lose himself quickly in this darkness, she relented. "Look. I'm sorry. I'll be nicer. I'm just scared. But whatever happens, we can't get split up? We have to stay together. Hey, do you have a belt on?"

"Yes," he said. "Why?"

"Take it off," she commanded.

"Uh . . ."

"We can snake it through each of our belt loops, weirdo. That way we know where the other person is. You know, just in case."

"Oh," his voice said, as if that made perfect sense.

Awkward didn't even begin to cover the process. Heads bumped, Litney fell over twice, and it took Dokken forever to get the belt fastened since he had to do it entirely by feel. "Man," Dokken exclaimed when they were finally connected. "That seemed to take as much effort as the fifty push-ups Mr. Fitch makes us do in gym every day."

Taking a deep breath, Litney nodded. Realizing Dokken couldn't see her response, she said, "Yeah, I know. Okay, so which way should we go?"

"Oh, I'd say *North by Northwest*."

"Ha ha."

"Hitchcock, you know," he said with a grin in his voice. "He's one of my favorite movie directors of all time."

"Great, now how about we focus on what we are doing?"

"No need to get all snotty about it," he retorted.

"In case you haven't noticed, we're screwed. We're in absolute dark, we have no idea where we are or what we should do. Excuse me if I don't think now is a good time for obscure movie references."

"It's not a good time for attitude either," he muttered.

Ignoring him, Litney said, "We might as well head in the direction we're facing. Ready? Let's go."

The two of them began to crawl on their hands and knees through what felt like nice soft grass. It wasn't long before Dokken said, "I feel like we're playing horsey out in the backyard." With that he gave a big loud, "Neigh!"

Litney shushed him. "We don't want to draw any more attention to ourselves than we—what was that?" She froze.

Dokken, who didn't realize she had stopped moving, kept crawling, making Litney face-plant on the ground when the belt jerked her forward.

"Dokken!" she ground out, pulling back hard on the belt. This time it was Dokken's turn to land face first in the grass.

"Hey, you didn't need to do that. How was I supposed to know you had stopped moving?"

"Would you be quiet?" she whispered fiercely. "I heard something."

When the two of them quit talking, the dark was as quiet as it was dark. "I don't hear anything," he whispered. "What did it sound like?"

"It was this tiny squeaking," she answered.

"What, like a mouse?"

"No, like something that needed oil."

"But, but that would be a good thing, wouldn't it?" his excited voice asked. "It could be a house or a place . . . with lights and a door, with a lock on it."

"Or," she countered, "it could be where the Ignitatus lives, a place where we get locked in with no chance of ever getting out."

"So . . . what do we do?"

Litney considered the alternatives aloud. "If we stay where we are, something could attack us."

"Or we could die from thirst and starvation," Dokken pointed out.

She sighed. "Yes, if we didn't move for ten days, we could die from thirst and starvation. If we move toward the sound, something could attack us."

"Or we could find a nice little house with a big old light switch."

Her sigh was bigger this time. "If we go away from the squeaking noise and head in a different direction, then . . ."

"Then what?" he asked.

"I don't know. What are we going to do?" she bemoaned.

"Look, why don't we go toward the noise."

"Why?" she asked.

"Because it is better to go toward something than to wander away into nothing."

"But—"

"I know," he interrupted, but his voice was consoling. "It's terrifying either way. It's just that something's telling me to go toward the sound. Which way was it coming from? Why don't you lead, nice and slowly so we don't crash again, and I'll follow."

For a moment, Litney felt like a snowman, frozen to the spot without any hope of ever moving—she was so afraid. Then she said, "How stupid."

"Look," Dokken said, his voice sounding angry, "I don't think we have any other choice."

"Not that. We need light," she whispered.

"No, duh—" Dokken started to say when suddenly a small light gleamed in the darkness. "But, how?"

"My bracelet. I was so scared I forgot all about it."

Dokken laughed. "Me, too." He looked at Litney's face in the soft light. Boy, she was pretty. Glad it wasn't light enough for her to see the shade of red he was certain his face had just become, he cleared his throat and said, "I still think we should go toward the squeaking sound."

"Yes," she whispered. "This way."

"Hey, we could stand up now," Dokken suggested and started undoing the belt that connected the two of them. "This grass is nice and soft, so crawling isn't horrible, but if we go slow, it would probably be a lot easier if we were on our feet."

"You're right. Here, let me help you up," she offered him her hand. He hesitated only a second before taking it.

They did not have to walk very far before they found what was making the noise. When Dokken reached out a hand to touch it, he said, "It's metal. Point your bracelet upward. I think it goes up pretty high."

After she had focused the light above them, she said, "Can you tell what it is? It reminds me of windmills I've seen on old farmsteads. Except . . . except I don't see any fan blades. It looks more like a funnel up there, doesn't it?"

"Yeah, like something pours into it, but not from the top, from the side. What do you think it is?"

"I don't know," Litney said. Then she gave a little cough. "That's weird. I've got a tickle in my chest."

"Me, too," Dokken admitted. "And my head doesn't feel so good. It's like it's hard to breathe."

Litney found herself struggling to take a full breath, and her head began to spin. The sensations got worse and more frightening, and just as she was about to black out, a horrible creature rushed at her from out of the dark and screamed at her, "Are ye insane?"

She tried to scream, sure that she had just met a Breath Bandit or the Ignitatus, but she didn't have any air left. Then the creature did the unthinkable—it not only blocked the light from the bracelet, but it also put its lips to hers.

"Stop . . ." Dokken breathed heavily, trying to pull the creature off of her, but he was too weak, and he couldn't see very well anymore. It was like his brain was in a blender. All his thoughts were whirling and being sucked down, and he couldn't get any of his limbs to obey him. But he was aware enough to see that the creature had dropped Litney and so the bracelet was shining softly once more. That's how he could see the creature was now turning toward him, coming straight for his mouth. Maybe it was a zombie, and it was going to eat his brains, or some evil spirit about to suck the life right out of him. The world was just about gone when he felt the creature's lips touch his own.

"HEY, WHO ARE YOU?" DOKKEN DEMANDED, when he came to again.

"Shut those loud mouths of yers!" the owner of the voice hissed. "Now, follow me."

"But we can't se—" Litney began, realizing that this creature had a hold of her wrist with what felt like a huge hand, and this hand was covering any light the bracelet might be offering.

"Be quiet!" came the harsh whisper. "I will lead ye."

In the black darkness Litney and Dokken were pulled to their feet and dragged forward. They did not walk very long before stopping. It was only because it was so quiet that they could hear the tiniest squeak, and then they were pulled forward again. Their wrists were released, they heard the squeak again, six clicks, and finally a scraping sound. A few seconds later, a soft glow appeared. They were in a room and several candles had been lit.

"Who are ye stupid creatures, then?" the voice asked in an angry lilt.

Litney gasped. Not at the creature's words, but at his battered face and body. The creature had the same falcon-like head as the Gadlanders above, except one eye was missing and a patch of rough pink skin had grown over where it should have been. And the mantle of feathers around its neck wasn't gorgeous or full as it had been with the other creatures. Instead, this creature's neck looked as if most of the left side and some of the right had been roughly plucked. There were even leftover shafts jutting out where the feathers ought to have been. One of his powerful legs was wrapped in a dirty bandage that had a dark-blue stain on it and a similar bandage was wrapped around each forearm.

"O, that's right," he sneered, seeing her reaction. "Be horrified by the ugly creature. Don't ye know that ye could have ended up looking like this? Didn't they tell ye about the Breath Bandits and the Ignitatus up there?" He jerked his head upward.

"Yes, yes," Dokken said, trying to look at this creature without pity or horror. He couldn't tell yet if this mangled Gadlander was friend or foe, but Dokken knew he didn't want to make the creature angry. Or at least any angrier than he already was. "But we're not from here. We don't know what they are. In fact, I kind of thought ye were a Breath Bandit or an Ignitatus."

"No, I'm not, but yer mighty lucky, ye crazy dolts, that I got there when I did. Ye may as well have been shouting, 'Here I am. Come and get me!' Not only were ye loud, but ye had that light." He narrowed his one eye and checked them over. "Where was it coming from?"

Litney hesitated, but then she thought it was safe to say, "My bracelet. It can give off light."

"The Breath Bandits are drawn to heat and light, so it was easy for them to find ye, easy for them to crawl down yer throat and go into yer lungs. Didn't ye feel them getting rid of every last bit of breath ye had?"

"Yes," Litney said with a shudder. "How do they crawl down your throat? Wouldn't you gag and throw up?"

"Breath Bandits have bodies made of smoke. That's why it's so hard to tell if they are around. They don't make any noise, and ye can walk right through them. The only way ye know they're there is if ye start to feel a tickle at the very bottom of yer lungs. If ye do, ye have only fifteen seconds to get rid of them."

"We felt that, didn't we?" Dokken asked Litney.

She nodded, grateful that this creature had found them before it had been too late.

"But how do you get rid of them?"

"There's a good way and a horrible way," the creature answered.

"What's the good way?" Litney asked.

"Someone has to kiss you."

"That's what you were doing!" Litney exclaimed. "I thought you were trying to suck my brains out."

"Me, too," Dokken said with a smile. "But that's stupid. How in the world could kissing do anything?"

With his one good eye, the creature glared at the boy. "It's not stupid. It's survival. I don't know how it works, just that it does. It draws them out somehow. Kind of like heat does to an infection."

"So what's the horrible way?" Litney asked. Looking at the creature, she had a feeling she already knew.

"You have to make them want to leave."

"And how do you do that? By hurting *yourself*?" she whispered.

The creature gave one curt nod.

"Wait," Dokken interrupted, putting up both his hands and shaking his head. "You mean to tell me that *you*, *you* did all that to *yourself*?"

The Gadlander gave another sharp nod.

"You mean, *you* plucked out *your* own eye?" Dokken shifted his gaze to the door. Anyone capable of doing that was also probably capable of doing them a great deal of harm. They needed to get out of here. Now.

"No, I did not do that. That was the Ignitatus."

"What is the Ignitatus?" Litney asked, trying to mask how horrified she was by all of this.

"The Ignitatus is where the Breath Bandits come from. Ye see, its body is made entirely of fire, and while it can gallop across the land burning everything in its path, most of the time it just sits and guards the entrance to the bror mine."

"The bror mine?" Dokken repeated, and for the first time, he looked around the room. There was the door they had come in—with a row of six huge locks bolting them inside—and there were no windows on any of the walls. The room was about the size of his bedroom at home, and there was one bed along the far wall, a rocking chair, a small tub on a stand and a row of ten or twelve pots, each containing different kinds of plants with different kinds of brightly colored flowers.

"Bror is one of the things that Gad is famous for," the Gadlander answered. "It is a substance that has qualities of reflection."

"You mean like a mirror?" Litney clarified. She, too, took in their surroundings and decided this creature must have a small life.

"Sort of. What's special about it is it reflects its surroundings. It—" The creature stopped, obviously stuck in how to describe it. He asked, "Do ye have creatures on yer planet that can disappear into environments?"

The chameleon immediately popped into Litney's head. "Yes. We have something called a chameleon that can change colors to match whatever environment it's in. So if it's on a tree branch, it'll be brown. If it's among the leaves, it'll turn green."

"That's what bror does," the creature said, nodding. "Whoever holds a piece of it is able to blend into their surroundings. They can still be seen, if someone looks hard enough. But to those who aren't paying attention, it's almost as if the one holding the bror has become invisible."

A line formed between Dokken's eyebrows as he tried to think about this. "But why would this Ignitatus guard it? Is it that special?"

"For years, it was nothing more than what we used to sneak past the kwits . . . ah, the creatures who guard the flowers." With a jerk of his head, he indicated the flowers in the pots over by the sink. "Kwits are the size of my arm and they have stingers as long as my fingers." The creature held up his index finger which was at least five inches long. "They're able to fly, and so they hover over the flower fields, trying to keep us from picking them. But since we eat the flowers, we needed to find a way to sneak past the kwits. We used bror."

"But that doesn't sound like any reason for the Ignitatus to guard the mine. Unless he wanted you to starve," Dokken observed, wandering over to look at the flowers. One plant had yellow flowers with blue streaks on it. Another was pure purple. Some flowers were long and thin, others wide and open.

"The Ignitatus would like it if I starved, but no, he guards the bror because another has become interested in it."

"What's your name?" Litney asked suddenly. "I'm Litney, and this is Dokken."

"My name is Roonan," the creature answered, putting his right hand to the middle of his chest.

"Thank you, Roonan, for saving us," Litney said with a small smile. "I don't know what we would have done without you."

"Ye would have died," Roonan pronounced, and Litney nodded her agreement to that frightening fact.

"You said that someone else has become interested in the bror. Is it the king?" Dokken inquired, bending down to smell the yellow flower. Since he had lived in a big city most of his life, Dokken had never really had a chance to see many flowers, at least not up close. Sure, he had seen and smelled roses, but a carnation was probably the only other kind of flower he had actually touched. So when he put this blossom up to his nose, he didn't have much to compare its scent to. Still, he doubted any flower on earth smelled like this. It was as if light had traveled up his nose, jumped all the way down into his belly and then ricocheted back up directly into his brain. He wouldn't have admitted this if his life depended on it, but he felt all warm and gooey inside. Without thinking, he murmured, "Wow."

Roonan chuckled. "Amazing, isn't it? That's from the real Gad. Not that, that travesty up there. That is *not* Gad. At least not the Gad I grew up with. The Gad I grew up with had rivers and flowers and trees and boulders. We lived in huts with wheat growing on the roofs. If we wanted bread, all we had to do was climb up the ladder on the back of the house, cut some wheat, grind it, and bake it. Do you know how wonderful that tasted? Can you imagine? You asked if it was the king who is interested in the bror. The answer is yes and no. Yes, because it was the king who built all of that over Gad. He wanted people to forget about bror and that way of life. He wanted people to forget what we had, because there is someone, or some *thing*, else who is after the bror, and the king and the Ignitatus work for this other."

"Who?" asked Litney, who had now joined Dokken over by the flowers. She smelled a royal blue one, and it made her feel like she was on a merry-go-round at the park. There was afternoon sunshine on her face while her insides laughed and twirled. "Oh, my," she whispered.

"I don't know who it is," Roonan replied as he stood watching them.

"So how do you know there is this other?" Dokken asked, looking at the other flowers. He wasn't sure if he wanted to smell them or not. While the amazing feeling of the yellow flower still fluttered through him, he didn't know if he wanted to find out what the other blossoms did to him.

"Because I have heard them," the lilting voice replied. "That thing ye were looking at out there, it is what I use to listen for them, to them. I know the king's voice, and I have had the misfortune of hearing the Ignitatus's voice saying to me, 'I will burn you to death, piece by piece by piece,' as his tail of fire gouged out one of my eyes."

Litney gasped and Dokken shuddered as if he had just received a hundred paper cuts.

An indifferent Roonan continued, "There are times when I hear a third voice, talking to them, commanding their every move."

"Do you know why this voice wants the bror? Have you heard it say?" Litney asked, pointing at the rocking chair as if to ask Roonan's permission for her to sit down.

The creature swept his big hand toward the chair and waited until Litney had made herself comfortable before he continued. "It has never said why it wants the bror. All I know is it wants the bror and some liquid. I have spent hours trying to figure out what the voice might be referring to, but I can't imagine what kind of liquid it could be."

Dokken's eyes found Litney's.

Apparently the one eye Roonan had left was a shrewd one, because he demanded of the two kids, "What do ye know?"

Dokken stuttered, "N-nothing. We don't know anything about a magical liquid."

Litney shook her head because she knew what was coming. Roonan pointed out, "I didn't say it was a magical liquid, did I?" Leaning toward the two of them, he said, "Ye will tell me what ye know. Now."

"We don't know all that much more," she said. And when she saw the Gadlander didn't believe her, she said, "No, really. We don't. We're from another place—"

"I worked that one out for meself," Roonan said wryly.

"And we were brought here against our will. We—"

Dokken interrupted her to make a blunt observation. "We don't know if we can trust you. How do we know you aren't working for the king up there? How do we know this isn't all a setup? Throw us in the dark and scare the bejeebers out of us after the liquid didn't work because then we'll tell the truth. No. We aren't going to tell you."

In one swift movement, Roonan stormed over to the door and began unlocking the locks. He wrenched the door open, then crossed the room to grab each of them by the wrist. Pulling them toward the gaping black, he said, "Fine. Don't tell me. But then ye aren't staying in my house. Get out!"

Litney and Dokken felt themselves being tossed out the door and back into the darkness, which was now even more terrifying because they knew what was out there waiting for them. As they listened to each and every one of Roonan's locks being slipped back into place, Litney said, "Light," and the bracelet accommodated her by giving off its quiet glow. Then she turned on Dokken and demanded, "What did you do that for? After hearing all of that about the Breath Bandits, after seeing what the Ignitatus did to his eye, you really thought it better to be back out here than to tell him what we know?"

"Shhhh!" Dokken hissed since her voice had grown increasingly loud and shrill. "We don't want them to find us."

"They wouldn't have found us if we had stayed inside with Roonan," Litney said harshly, though she did return her voice to a whisper. "We need to knock, and you need to apologize."

"But—"

"No. Dokken, we don't know what's going on. We don't know what the magical liquid is, we don't know who the king and the Ignitatus are working for, we don't know anything at all about this world. In other words, we need Roonan. Now, knock."

* 10 *

"ARE YOU SERIOUS?" Dokken asked a while later when Roonan handed him a plate. The Gadlander had let them back inside only after extracting a promise from the two of them that they would tell him about the magical liquid. They had, and then Roonan had started puttering around the kitchen, saying they were probably hungry. When he had finally put a plate in each of their hands, Dokken had to admit that what was in front of him was very pretty, what with flowers thrown all over his meal. The problem was he didn't want pretty, he wanted huge. His body might not have grown big yet, but his appetite sure had. Back home his parents were probably eating lasagna right now, and he'd be on his third or fourth helping. Or maybe they had already finished hours ago, because who knew how long he and Litney had been gone at this point. Anyway, what was on the plate in front of him wasn't going to fill his right pinky, let alone his bottomless stomach.

"Dokken, we don't want to get thrown back outside," Litney said, both warning and humor in her voice. "Roonan, this is beautiful. Thank you for feeding us."

Dokken knew he should be keep his mouth shut and focus on being thankful. Instead he said, "You have to have something else. Another course coming? Or a huge stockpile of snacks in a cupboard somewhere, right? You're a big creature. There's no way you can survive off this."

Roonan blinked at him with his one good eye, but said nothing.

Dokken asked hopefully, "Can we at least get seconds?"

The Gadlander shook his head and said simply, "Eat."

Since there wasn't a table, Litney took a seat in the rocking chair, while Dokken and Roonan walked across the room to sit on the floor and lean against a bare wall. Dokken looked down at his plate once again. There was a lime green thing, no bigger than a golf ball a little to the right of the center of the plate. Then some sort of red stuff was drizzled into swirls on the rest of the white plate. Finally, six flowers were strewn here and there on the plate. Dokken reached for the yellow blossom he had smelled earlier. "Are these to eat?" he asked Roonan. After what the smell alone had done to him, he wanted to make sure eating it wasn't going to kill him in ten seconds flat. Roonan nodded, and Dokken paused with the flower at his lips for a moment. Deciding he was so hungry he had to have something, he ate it. Flavor roared through his mouth as delight pinged from elbow to ear, from neck to knee. His insides felt like he had been thrown out of an airplane and fallen through miles and miles of warm delicious sunshine. After he swallowed, he demanded, breathless, "What was that?"

"Ye must have eaten a flower," Roonan said, who had been enjoying his own meal. "What color was it?"

"Yellow and blue," Dokken answered.

"It's called Falling Light," Roonan told him. Then the Gadlander picked one of the yellow and blue blossoms off his own plate. After plopping it in his mouth, he closed his eyes and groaned. "Those are my favorites."

Dokken frowned at his plate. "Is every one of these flowers going to do that to me?"

"Do what to ye?" Roonan asked.

"I don't know . . . explode like that in me."

"No. There are a few more that will do something like that but most of them just feel like sun on yer tongue. Watch out for that orange one, though," Roonan warned, pointing at the tiniest blossom on his plate.

"Why? What's that one called?"

"Portentious Pucker."

"Portentious Pucker?" Dokken repeated. "But it's so small. It doesn't look like it could do much."

"It might be small, but it is so sour that one taste will make ye feel as if yer mouth is being sucked backward into yer stomach."

"Really?" Dokken mused, and he glanced at Litney, She was sitting far enough away from him and Roonan that it appeared she had not heard their exchange. Raising his voice a little, he asked her, "Have you tried any flowers yet?"

"Mmm hmm," she said, looking up. "A yellow one. Wow, it was like taking a ride on a roller coaster."

"Guess what it's called," he said smartly.

"I don't know. What?"

"Falling Light," he answered.

Litney smiled and murmured, "Perfect."

Dokken held out the petite orange blossom he had asked Roonan about and said, "Do you have one of these?"

Litney looked at his hand and then back down at her plate. "Yes, I do. Why? Aren't you going to eat it?"

He answered, "I don't know. Do you think I should try it?"

Litney picked up her orange blossom and said, "I can try it first if you want me to."

"Nah. I might be a bit afraid, but really I'm more curious." With that, he popped the flower into his mouth and sighed. "Oh, man."

"Good?"

"Mmmmmm."

"What's it like?" Litney wanted to know.

"You'll love it. It's like eating clouds spun out of sugar. I think it might be the sweetest thing I have ever eaten." He glanced at Roonan, who was trying to hide a smile.

Eagerly, Litney popped the blossom into her mouth. It wasn't like clouds spun out of sugar at all! It was like sucking on a lemon and then washing it down with a cup of pickle juice. She couldn't talk or even spit the beastly thing out, her mouth had puckered so hard. All she could do was swallow the flower as quickly as she could. "Bleck!" she finally exclaimed.

Dokken laughed at her and Roonan joined in. "Sorry to have a laugh at ye, miss," the creature said, still chuckling, "but the look on yer face."

"Ha ha, very funny," Litney muttered. "You're a big liar, Dokken Carver. What I want to know is how in the world could you make it look like that tasted good?"

"Because I love lemons, dill pickles, and excruciatingly sour candy, so for me, it really was delicious. Plus," he said, his eyes shining with glee, "as soon as it hit my tongue, I couldn't wait to see you chomp on it. Evil, huh?"

"Very," Litney tried to sound hurt, but her smile gave her away. She examined the remaining flowers on her plate. "Do we dare?"

Dokken smiled at her and was about to say something to Roonan when he noticed the Gadlander was watching the two humans with a hard, sad eye. "Is something wrong?"

"It's nothin'," the creature muttered, shaking his head and glaring at his plate.

"Are you sure? Is it something we did? Are you in pain?" Dokken pointed at the bandages on Roonan's body.

"Every night in Gad we used to have a feast," the Gadlander answered, his eyes still on the plate in his hands.

Dokken nodded, although he didn't have a clue why this would make the Gadlander appear sad and angry.

"We had what was called a Gathering Place, and every night, we would all show up with baskets of flower and all kinds of other food. The only time ye ate at home was when ye were too sick to leave the house. Otherwise we would all gather and eat and dance and listen to the music. The babes got to wrestle and shout and play without anyone telling them to behave. The young ones got to meet someone, maybe fall in love. The elders got to tell all the old stories and remember."

"It sounds delightful," Litney said when Roonan seemed to get lost in his thoughts.

His voice was hoarse when he whispered, "I haven't eaten with another creature in a very long time."

Dokken squirmed. What was he supposed to say to that? It's okay? It will happen again soon? Gee, how 'bout them flowers?

It was Litney who found the perfect thing to say. "Thank goodness Gad has you fighting for it."

"But that's what I don't understand," Roonan said, shaking his head.

"What do you mean?" Litney asked

"Why am I the only one fighting? It's horrible up there. Loud and bright and fake. Not one thing is real. Am I the only one who remembers what Gad used to be like, with its trees and flowers and rivers? Am I the only one who wants to live in that Gad until the day I die?"

Litney and Dokken remained silent. Neither had an answer for him.

"YE STILL WANT MORE?" ROONAN, who seemed to have cheered up some, asked Dokken.

Dokken looked down at his empty plate and shook his head with a smile. "I don't get it. How can some flowers and a thing the size of a golf ball fill me up? But it did. I couldn't eat another bite if I tried."

"I thought ye'd say that," Roonan said as he took their dishes and put them in the sink. Turning back toward them, he declared, "Now, we need to decide what we're going to do. I'd rather take some time to think about this, but since ye are concerned for yer friends up there, it appears we need to make some decisions and fast. Ye said the magic liquid worked back in your world, but that it didn't work here."

"Right," Dokken said, nodding.

"But yer sure that ye brought the right thing?"

"As sure as we can be. We searched the entire property and couldn't find anything else."

"And the tea ye drank," Roonan said, pointing at Litney, "what did it do to ye?"

"It's hard to explain," Litney said, throwing her hands up. "It made me feel strong and powerful. Certain."

"So why would someone be after it? Feeling strong and powerful doesn't seem to be so much. I suppose the question is were ye strong and powerful or did ye only feel that way?"

"I honestly don't know. It wasn't like I tried to lift the kitchen table or anything."

"And why the bror and the liquid?" Dokken mused as he sat down in the rocking chair Litney had just vacated so she could start pacing. "And who is it working with the king and the Ignitatus?"

"I'm in the dark," Roonan said with a grin, and the other two groaned at his pun.

"Since we don't know anything, what do we do?" Litney lamented. "Go back up and deal with the king? Stay down here and face the Ignitatus? How can we figure out who this other is?"

Roonan opened his mouth to answer her, but then he snapped it shut.

"What were you going to s—" Litney started to ask.

"Hush!"

The silence that followed allowed them to hear a faint tapping sound.

Her eyes round with fear, Litney pointed, as if to ask, "Is that your door?"

Roonan shook his head and walked over to a table with a box on it. The box had wires coming out of it that disappeared into the wall, and Litney realized that must be how Roonan listened to the Ignitatus.

A scuffling noise now came out of the box and then a voice asked, "May I enter?"

"The king," Dokken mouthed to Litney.

She nodded, because she had also recognized the voice.

"You may if you have good news," a voice that sounded like fingernails on a chalkboard drawled.

"The Ignitatus?" Litney whispered to Roonan as she rubbed at the goosebumps that had risen on her arm.

Roonan shook his head and held up three fingers. It was the third voice, then, the one he didn't know.

The scuffling noise stopped, and several silent seconds ticked by. "I have news," the king replied, his voice was soft and slick, like it was trying to glide over something.

"I can kill him now if *you'd* like," a hoarse voice observed, and Roonan nodded before they had even asked the question. Yes, *that* voice belonged to the Ignitatus.

There was another pause. Finally, the voice, that didn't belong to anyone they knew, answered, "Let him enter. We will let him speak in his defense. Then *you* can kill him."

This time, instead of goosebumps, Litney shivered. That voice . . . it did something to her.

"I understand *you* will think I have failed," the king began.

"Do *you* have the liquid?" the unknown voice inquired.

"Well, *you* see—"

"Do . . . *you* . . . have . . . it?" the voice interrupted.

"No."

"Then *you* have failed." With that, the voice let out a harrowing frustrated scream, and in that moment, Litney knew an awful truth. Her terrified and confused eyes looked to Dokken for confirmation. She couldn't believe it when he stared back at her blankly, that is until she recalled he didn't remember. He didn't remember a thing about their last adventure, and that included the creature who had killed him in a cave. But Litney could remember it. She could remember it all—his cold body, the sand, her tears.

⁂ 11 ⁂

SHE KNEW WHO THE THIRD voice belonged to—it was Mala. Dokken and Roonan were listening so intently to the conversation unfolding between the three voices that they didn't notice when Litney wrapped her arms tightly around her middle and sank to her knees.

"At least tell me you have the two humans," Mala hissed when she had gotten herself back under control.

"Yes," the king sounded relieved to be able to answer affirmatively. "Yes, we have them, but they aren't talking either. The man, he especially—"

"The man?" Mala interrupted. "You mean the *boy*, right?"

"Uh, what do you mean?" the king responded after a beat. "I have the big tall man. It's his farm where the magic liquid is. As I was saying, he is especially—"

Mala screamed again, and it was then that Dokken noticed Litney huddled on the floor. He rushed over to her and whispered in her ear, "What's wrong? Are you okay?"

She shook her head, then replied, "No, I'm not okay, but I'll tell you about it when they're done talking."

His face showed concern, but he nodded and didn't say anything more. He sat down on the ground beside her.

"No, not that man, not him. I want the boy. The red-haired boy and the girl with him. Did she have a bracelet on?"

If Dokken's face had shown concern before, now it showed a combination of confusion and fear. "How—?" he began, but again, Litney shook her head. They had to hear what was being said.

"You, you wanted *them*?" the king stuttered. "But they were just meant to deliver the liquid. They aren't important . . . are they?"

There was a thud followed by an anguished moan.

"Listen, you idiot," came Mala's voice. "You have failed and failed. Tell me where the boy and the girl are or you will die."

"D-d-down here somewhere. I had them thrown down here when the liquid didn't work. Please, don't hurt me."

"Was the girl wearing a bracelet?" Mala demanded.

"I d-don't . . . uh, maybe. Maybe she was. She could have been."

Mala growled, but since there weren't any more groans of pain, she must not have taken her frustration out on the king again. Instead, she simply asked, "Can you find them?"

It appeared that question had not been directed to the king, because it was the Ignitatus' smoky voice that answered. "Yes, I can. And what would you like me to do to them when I find them? Kill them?"

"Not yet. I believe they have something I want."

"The liquid?" the Ignitatus asked.

"No. A bracelet. Now go. And bring them back here as quickly as possible. Wait," Mala said in a low voice. "If you can't bring them both back, kill the boy. But bring me the girl. Do you understand? Bring me the girl."

"This can't be happening," Litney moaned, her arms wrapped tightly around her knees as she rocked on the floor. "How is this happening?"

"Do you know what's going on?" Dokken asked, sitting up on his knees and staring intently at her face. "The third voice said the Ignitatus could kill me, but not you. Why? Why am I the one who has to get killed? Again!"

"Seems ye all have some more explaining to do," Roonan said, standing over the two of them, his body tight with anger. "Ye know far more than ye let on, don'cha? What were ye doing, gathering information from me so ye could destroy me? Destroy any last hopes I had of helping restore Gad? Stand up! Explain!"

Litney recoiled at his sharp tone, but he reached one of his huge hands under her armpit and dragged her to her feet. "Roonan, sir, you're hurting my arm. I'll tell you what is going on, even though it's almost unbelievable, incredible. But you have to let me go or I won't talk."

The Gadlander released her arm and stood there waiting.

Litney paused, because she wasn't sure where to start her story. She decided to start at the beginning. "Do you see this?" she held up her bracelet to Roonan. "It's a magical bracelet that comes to all the women in my family. A couple of months ago, it came to me, but I got it earlier than I should have. That's because an evil force wanted the bracelet, and the only way she could get it was to take it from me. I went to another world, and came face to face with this evil creature. Her name was Mala." She hesitated and swallowed. "That third voice, the one you don't know? That was Mala." Her eyes slid to Dokken and watched this information sink in.

"The same Mala? The one who already killed me once?" he asked, his face turning as pale as a white bed sheet. "Are you sure?"

"What do ye mean, already killed ye once?" Roonan demanded.

"While we were in that other world, Dokken died. I had never met him before, but he joined me in that world as we tried to stop Mala, and well, she killed him."

"But how is that possible?" Roonan said, shaking his head.

"What is even weirder is that not only did Dokken die while we were there, but so did Mala. She had gotten the bracelet from me, we struggled and fell into a river, and then I, I killed her because she was trying to kill me. I thought the bracelet was lost. It disappeared in that river, and no matter how hard I tried, I couldn't find it. I thought I had lost it forever." Litney's voice shook, but she stood up now, tall and dry-eyed.

"So how did ye get the bracelet back?"

"I wished for it when we were going back home after our first visit here. When we got back, it was on my wrist."

"How did Dokken join ye this time?" Roonan's one eye bored into her.

"He moved to the town where I live. We met in school and have been friends ever since. The people we're trying to save, Talmoon and Pansy, they live out behind his house. Look, I know it sounds crazy and it doesn't make any sense, but it's the truth. I didn't tell you any of it because I didn't think it had anything to do with what was going on now."

Roonan thought for a moment. "Why is the bracelet so important to this Mala? And what does it have to do with the bror and the magical liquid ye were telling me about?" An agitated Roonan started to pace back and forth in the room.

Litney sighed and tried to think of the quickest way to explain all of this to Roonan. "The bracelet's powerful in its own right. It can grant requests . . . like the light you saw out there." She pointed at the door. "It was so dark, I asked it to give us some light, and it did. But I don't think that's the reason Mala's after it. She told me it can also act like a key and this key is very powerful. It lets whoever wears it into any world at any time. And that's important because different creatures gain different powers in different worlds. If she could get into all these different worlds quickly, she could get really powerful . . . and really dangerous."

"What do ye mean gain different powers?"

"Like in that other world, Dokken could read my mind." She paused, then asked Dokken, "Can you do that here?"

"Nope. I tried earlier when the king was questioning us, because I was wishing I could, but I can't."

"So what can ye do in this world?" Roonan asked, eyeing Dokken.

"I don't know. I haven't discovered anything yet."

"And what about ye? What can ye do?"

"I don't know either."

"If this bracelet is so powerful, why don't ye use it? Tell it to kill Mala and the king and the Ignitatus. Make it work for us. Help me free Gad."

Litney grabbed herself around the middle again and admitted quietly, "I'm afraid to try that, because I don't know how to use the bracelet all that well. I don't want to make things worse."

Roonan glared at her, then turned away, muttering, "So the bracelet is useless to us, even though this Mala wants it so badly, she's willing to destroy my world for it."

Dokken walked over to the wall where he had eaten his dinner and slid down it, pulling his knees up and resting his head on them as he did so.

"You okay?" Litney whispered, standing above him.

He didn't answer, just shook his head.

"What are you thinking?" she pleaded. "You've got to talk to me."

His blue eyes found her brown ones, "I'm thinking I'm about to die again. I'm thinking this scares the . . . well, the you know what out of me. I'm thinking I don't want to stay imprisoned in this hut for the rest of my life, but I sure as heck don't want to step out that door, because the Ignitatus is coming for me."

"No, the Ignitatus is coming for me," Litney corrected him. "Mala wants me and the bracelet."

Narrowing his eyes, Dokken said through his clenched jaw, "But the Ignitatus wasn't given directions to kill *you*. In fact," he said more loudly, "the Ignitatus was given directions *not* to kill you. The same thing can't be said for me!"

"Dokken," Litney said in a soothing voice. "I'm not trying to get into a fight over who should be more scared right now, okay? I think we both have some pretty darn good reasons to be terrified. But we can't start fighting each other. I need you to help me."

"What if I don't want to help you?" he asked, pulling at his shoe string and avoiding her eyes. Then suddenly, he looked right at her and demanded, "What if I want to stay in here where it is safe? Does that make me a bad person? Does that make me a coward?"

Taking a deep breath, she whispered, "I would understand. You went through something horrible, something I didn't. I think if it had happened to me, I'd be feeling the same way you are right now." She stood over him a moment longer, waiting to see if he was going to say anything else. When he didn't, she decided it was best to give him some time and space. She turned and approached Roonan. "Can you lead me to where the bror is? It sounds as if the Ignitatus won't be there, so if you could show me where it is, I could get this over with Mala."

"But ye don't know what she wants," Roonan pointed out.

"Not specifically. I don't know what the liquid is or what it has to do with the bror, but I do know she still wants the bracelet. It seems like she isn't going to rest until that happens." A small wry smile flashed across Litney's face. "Or it seems like she isn't going to stay dead until that happens."

"I don't understand how this is happening," Roonan admitted. "Around here, dead is dead." Then he pointed to the ceiling, "Was she the one behind building all of that over Gad?"

Litney shrugged. "I don't know. Maybe. Again, I don't think we'll ever know all that's going on. But what matters is that Talmoon and Pansy are still up there, and they need our help. And you need my help. And Gad does, too. So I'm asking, will you lead me to where Mala is? I'm not asking you to help me fight her, but I can't get there on my own. I need your help."

"Yes. I'll help ye." With his one good eye, he glanced at the boy sitting on the floor.

"I don't think he'll be coming," Litney explained. Before the Gadlander could say what he thought of this, she continued, "and I can't blame him."

Roonan gave a single, slow nod. "I have a few things to pack, and then we can go."

"How long does it take to get there?" she asked.

"About an hour."

As Roonan was about to turn and walk away, Litney stopped him. "Hey, I've been wanting to ask, how does that thing work? Is it a radio?" She was pointing to the box the voices had come from.

"Radio?" Roonan repeated.

"It's something we have in our world . . . there are sound waves in the air and the radio kind of catches them and then we can hear things, like voices and music."

Scratching his head, the Gadlander repeated, "Sound waves? You mean like waves water can make? Do you have to duck out of the way of these waves as they fly through the air?"

She laughed. "No. They're invisible. Is that how your box works?"

"No, there's another rock, like the bror, but this one is far rarer. It lets you listen to things when you aren't there, but only if you can find one sirihiri rock and one hirisiri rock."

"Sirihiri rock? Hirisiri rock?" Litney asked in the exact same way as Roonan had said radio and sound waves.

"They are opposite rocks, and they have this attraction."

"Kind of like magnets, I bet," Litney said under her breath.

Roonan shrugged, "I don't know about . . . what did *ye* call them? Magnets? But these rocks, no matter how far apart they are, they always know where the other one is. And if *ye* have one, *ye* can hear what's going on wherever that other rock is. So outside in that thing *ye* were looking at is one rock, and for safety reasons, I designed this box so I could hear what was going on without having to stand outside. I put the other inside the cave with the Ignitatus."

"Wasn't that dangerous?" Litney gasped.

Roonan pointed to his missing eye in answer.

"Maybe we should wait and think about what we want to do some more," Litney said, her voice unsteady.

"No. I want my world back, and if that means dealing with this Mala, then that's what we're going to do. We'll be leaving in five minutes," he paused and glanced at Dokken, "so if *ye* need to say anything, do it now."

⁕ 12 ⁕

IT FELT WRONG, LEAVING DOKKEN BEHIND, hearing him slide the locks quietly back into place after the door closed. He hadn't said anything, hadn't looked at her, even when she had said, "Dokken, I'd really like to talk." He had just shaken his head and pointed toward the door where Roonan had been waiting for her.

Litney told herself Dokken had made his choice, and she couldn't think about him anymore right now. Now she had to concentrate on the task ahead. With this thought, her hand squeezed the rope even more tightly. Roonan had wrapped one end of it around his waist and then tied the other to her belt loop. "Once we get out there, we can't talk. Period," he had warned her. "Ye'll have to follow me, no matter what. If ye need me to stop, then give two tugs of the rope. Got it?" She had nodded, but she hadn't planned on it being so frightening, being led like a horse through the utter darkness. Not surprisingly, all sorts of frightening thoughts began to rush into her mind—things like getting separated from Roonan, Breath Bandits crawling in her lungs, and wondering what they were going to do once they arrived at the cave. They hadn't really had time to plan things out. She and Roonan hadn't gotten any further than, "We'll decide what to do when we get there."

As Litney felt herself being pulled along, she tried to distract her jittery thoughts with the scents that her nose caught now and again. Some of them smelled like a couple of those blossoms they had eaten for dinner, and she wondered what could be producing them since there wasn't any sun or light. How long had Gad been in the dark? All that could grow back home in the dark was mushrooms and maybe some moss, but neither of those smelled like what she was passing through now. She wished she could ask Roonan about it, but she remembered the look in his one good eye when he had told her there would be no talking. The last thing she wanted to do was to draw the Breath Bandits or Ignitatus to where they were, just because she wanted to know what she was smelling and how it was still growing.

So far, the land had been flat and soft. What felt like feathers brushed against her hands every once in a while; Litney guessed it was some kind of long grass. She had worried that the shushing sound their feet made as they walked would easily be heard, but there was a wind from somewhere making the grass all around them rustle. That made it hard to hear the sound of their feet going through the grass—at least she hoped that was the case.

The longer she walked, the more uncomfortable Litney grew. Usually, she didn't mind walking. Many summer evenings she would join her parents as they walked around their neighborhood. There was always something to see, and if there wasn't, at least there was always something to talk about—a book they had read, a story in the newspaper, what would be ready to eat from the garden soon. But as she continued to follow Roonan in complete silence and darkness, Litney began to feel weirder and weirder, as if she had floated away from reality somehow, as if she was now hovering in some kind of purgatory—neither dead nor alive, just stuck walking in the dark for the rest of time. To make sure she was still alive, she flicked her cheek. *Ouch*, she thought. *Okay, good. Still alive. But close to going insane. How much longer are we going to keep walking? But do I want to stop walking, because when we stop walking, we are at the cave where Mala is, and then what are we going to do? Roonan said I should just kill her with the bracelet. Sounds like a good idea. She's evil, and obviously she isn't going to stop until she gets the bracelet, but can I really just wish her dead? Would I want to even if I could? Seems kind of unfair, like that old saying of stabbing someone in the back. But do I want to face her again, because the last time I did, she was able to get the bracelet from me. She lost it in the end, but still. I wish Dokken was here.*

Her thoughts were interrupted by two tugs on the rope, but she was so wrapped up in what was going on in her head that she forgot that meant she was supposed to stop. Roonan gave a little grunt when she ran into the back of him. She opened her mouth to apologize, but then remembered speaking was strictly forbidden.

While she was glad to have stopped walking, Litney felt her fear and frustration mount. Now what were they supposed to do? Stand in the pitch black and wish Mala would evaporate back to her own planet and be stuck there forever? Would that work?

Suddenly, she felt a hand on her arm. She was about to scream until she realized it was Roonan's. He was patting his way up her arm, to her shoulder, to her head. Then both of his hands grasped her head and turned it to the right. There she saw a small light flickering in what looked like an open mouth. It must be the cave where Mala was. With his hands still on her head, she nodded. She hoped he could figure out she meant, "I see. I understand."

His hand patted its way down her arm again and found her hand. Gripping it, he pulled her, and as they started to walk, it occurred to Litney that another cliche applied disturbingly well—they were walking toward the light.

WHEN THEY CAME TO STOP about thirty feet from the glowing cave, Litney rubbed at her wrist, the one Roonan had been holding to lead her along. She felt the bracelet under her fingers. That's why it was so sore—Roonan's grip had made the metal dig into her flesh.

The bracelet . . . if only she could think of something to do with it. She had decided she wouldn't send out death vibes to Mala from the bracelet, but what could she do? Transport them directly into the cave? No. While it would give them the element of surprise, she wanted to do everything she could to avoid a direct confrontation with Mala.

A bubble would be nice, she thought. Some sort of barrier that hid them, so she could ask the bracelet for some light. And it would have to be soundproof, because then the two of them could talk and plan. She thought this over for a few moments and concluded she couldn't think of many dangers with this plan. Deciding to go for it, she figured she couldn't ask the bracelet out loud for either of these things, so she screwed up her face with concentration. It seemed odd to start out with her demand, so she began with, *Hi there, Bracelet. You have been so helpful in the past, and I am glad to have you with me right now. You know how dangerous Mala is. I wish you could give us a protective shield. One that makes it so we can't be seen once you turn on a light for us, and one that makes it so we can't be heard when we start talking. Can you do that for us, please? It would help us out a bunch.* All that was fine and good, but how was she supposed to know if it had worked or not? Should she simply hope the bracelet had done what she asked and start talking? She added, *If you could grow warm on my wrist to let me know you understand, to let me know when you've done what I asked, I would appreciate it.* Nothing happened. She waited another half a minute, vaguely wondering what Roonan was doing as the two of them stood there. He wasn't holding her wrist anymore, so what was he doing? She couldn't hear him, not even his breathing. Had he left her? She gave a tug on the rope. There was some resistance, so she assumed the two of them were still tied together. *Well, thank goodness I didn't try and kill Mala just by thinking about it,* she thought when the bracelet was still cold and inert on her wrist. *If I can't even get it to form a bubble over us, I sure couldn't get it to deal a fatal blow to Mala.* She paused, not sure if the bracelet was actually growing warm or if she had convinced herself it was growing warm because that's what she wanted to happen. After a few seconds more, though, she knew it was not her imagination. The bracelet was as warm as a piece of bread fresh from the oven. She could only hope that meant that the bubble was now around them.

"Light," she whispered.

"What are ye doing?!" Roonan whispered harshly, struggling to grab her wrist. "Put that out. Do ye want them to see us?"

"It's okay," Litney assured him. "No one can see or hear us right now."

His one eye glared at her as if she were not only reckless, but stupid.

"I'm serious. I wished the bracelet could create a shield for us—one that kept us invisible and was also soundproof."

"And how do ye know that this shield is over us?" Roonan asked, trying once again to cover the light from the bracelet with one of his huge hands.

"Because I told the bracelet to grow warm on my wrist when the shield was in place. Feel," she said, offering her wrist.

The Gadlander reached out, but it was only to cover the stone and throw them back into the dark. But he must have been able to tell it really was warm, because he removed his hand from the light and conceded. "And ye think that means it is working for you."

"Yes. I believe we are safe and can talk. We can figure out what to do now that we are here."

Roonan, whose body had naturally gone into a crouched position so he could fight or flee, relaxed and stood tall once again. "Ye will let me wear that bracelet and get rid of this Mala," he said, without preamble.

Litney considered this. When she had first received the bracelet, her mother had warned her several times that she could not take it off. Her mother had never told her what would happen if she did, but the way she had said it made it seem as if terrible consequences would occur if she removed the bracelet from her wrist. Did that apply here? How was she supposed to know? Something inside her told her, *The bracelet is yours to use. You must not take it off.* Staying with that feeling a few seconds more, to check and make sure it was right and real, she finally said, "No. I can't do that. The bracelet stays with me." Roonan opened his mouth to argue, but she stopped him. "Don't even try arguing with me. That's the way it is. So, what are we going to do?"

Roonan must have realized he wasn't going to change her mind, because he moved on by saying, "Do ye think this bubble would protect us all the way into the cave? We can't be seen and can't be heard, right? If the bubble can follow us, we can get into the cave, see what is going on and then decide from there."

She seemed hesitant when she said, "I don't know if it'll work or not. It seems like it should . . . why would the bubble give out right when we need it most?"

He must have heard the hesitancy in her voice, because Roonan asked, "Ye don't think it will?"

"I don't know . . . and the last thing I want to do is lead us into that cave and then have us standing there unprotected."

When she still failed to make a decision, he said, "Since this is the first time I've encountered the bracelet, I have no way of knowing what it will or won't do."

Litney took a deep breath. "I trust the bracelet. I trust that it will keep us protected. Let's go."

It did not take them long to cover the distance to the cave, and soon they were standing in front of it. "Please keep us protected," Litney whispered to the bracelet. When it grew warm on her wrist, she knew it had heard her and would do what she had asked. She and Roonan edged their way along one wall and stepped inside.

How hot it was in the cave! It reminded her of her great-grandmother's apartment in January—the heat was always on as high as it could go, and one time, Litney had forgotten to wear a short sleeve shirt. When huge embarrassing wet spots had appeared under her armpits, Litney's mother had taken pity on her. "I think I forgot something in the car," her mother had said loudly enough so her great-grandmother could hear. "Litney, would you help me go get it?" The two of them had found a bathroom downstairs, and her mother had given Litney her short-sleeved shirt and put on Litney's wet one. "Thanks, Mom," Litney had said, giving her a quick hug.

Now, Litney pulled her sweatshirt off and tied it around her waist, trying to figure out what the source of the heat was. There was a fire in the middle of the cave, but it was small. Since it felt as if an entire forest was burning that couldn't be where the heat was coming from. But before she could ask, Roonan declared, "It's empty."

"No, look," she said, pointing to the far back corner where a figure paced. Even though this creature looked like a Gadlander, she knew it wasn't. "That's Mala," she said.

"You never said Mala was a Gadlander," Roonan accused.

"She isn't. She can shape-shift."

"So how do you know this is Mala?"

"Because I remember her pacing around another cave. I recognize the way she holds herself, the way she walks."

"Why don't ye tell the bracelet to do something to her? Tie her up? Knock her out?" Roonan suggested as he watched Mala. "I'm as big as she is, but if she has any of those extra powers you were telling me about, I don't know if I could defeat her."

It sounded like a good idea. "Please knock Mala out so we can tie her up," she said to the bracelet. The figure pacing in the corner continued to pace. Not looking at Roonan, she said a little more loudly, "You have been so helpful. Could you please knock Mala out so we can tie her up?"

"No."

Litney jumped and Roonan said, "Now wait a minute. Did the bracelet just speak to ye?"

She nodded, her eyes wide.

"I'm guessing from yer reaction that it's never done that to ye before?"

Litney shook her head. "Not really. Last time I had it, when I was in a field, some voices from the bracelet told me how it had been created, but no, it's never talked to me, like in a conversation." She stared at the glowing stone on her wrist, and as if she were answering a telephone, said, "Hello?"

Silence.

She tried again. "I was just asking if you could knock Mala out, so we could—"

"No."

"No? Why not?"

"That is not a good wish," the bracelet responded.

"I'm not asking *you* to hurt her, just put her to sleep for a bit," Litney reasoned.

"No."

She sighed in exasperation. Wasn't the bracelet supposed to work for her? When did it decide to start telling her what she could do or not do? "So what will *you* do?"

Silence.

She met Roonan's eyes and mouthed, *Sorry*, then spent the next ten minutes trying out a variety of wishes on the bracelet—everything from, "Will *you* please whisk Mala back to her planet?" to "Will *you* make me as tall as the roof of the cave so I can tower over Mala and make her cower in fear?" Each wish was met with a simple and frustrating, "No."

"I've got it!" Roonan finally said, interrupting Litney just as she was asking if the bracelet would make Mala temporarily blind.

"What?" Litney asked, hoping he really did have something they could do. Otherwise, she was about to rip the bracelet off her wrist and throw it in the fire.

"See that?" he asked, pointing to the corner where Mala was still pacing. "Not Mala, but what is behind her?"

Straining her eyes, Litney thought she saw an opening. "Is that a tunnel? Another entrance?"

"It is what leads to the bror. We can sneak past Mala, get some bror, and then we will be invisible," Roonan declared.

"But we're invisible now," she pointed out.

"But we can't do anything to Mala. We're in this bubble. We need to get out of this bubble, but stay invisible. That way we could do something, like trip Mala and then tie her up."

"With what?" Litney asked.

Roonan tugged at the rope that still tied them together.

"We wouldn't be protected anymore," Litney observed.

"It would seem," he said, casting his eye at the bracelet, "that we can't do anything if we stay protected."

She didn't feel like she had any other choice, so Litney followed Roonan as they crept along the wall, closer and closer toward Mala. It was possible the creature heard them, or sensed them at least, because when they were within four feet of her (and within one foot of the door), she stopped pacing and stared directly at them. Litney clapped her hand to her mouth to stifle her gasp, believing, it seemed, that the bracelet's protection had given out. But it hadn't. After staring at the place where they were for a few more seconds, Mala began her pacing once again, muttering, "They will be found. They will be found. I will have it. I will have it."

They slipped into the tunnel and as they wound their way down, it grew even warmer, to Litney's dismay. The sweat that had kept to her hair up to this point began to run down her cheeks. "Why is it so warm in here?" she panted.

"The bror can only grow where there are hot steams," Roonan answered.

"How much farther is it?" she asked, wiping at her face with her shoulder.

"Right around this corner. Here," he said, gesturing across a cavern that was surprisingly large. Litney figured it was about half the size of the gymnasium at her school, and on the far side of it, something glowed faintly. As Roonan untied the two of them, he told her, "You can tell the bracelet thank you for the bubble, but we no longer need it."

Litney did so and the bracelet went cold and inert on her wrist. She followed Roonan as he crossed to the other side of the cavern and knelt down next to the pile of rocks that was glowing. She watched as he pulled a knife from the belt around his waist and began murmuring.

"What are you saying?" Litney whispered, looking back over her shoulder. This space was so big it made her feel unprotected.

"Bror can be dangerous . . . I have to make some of it want to come with me."

"What do you mean, dangerous?" Litney wanted to know, wiping her face with the sweatshirt around her waist. It was odd—every other cave she had ever been in had been cool and damp. This one felt like a huge sauna. "And . . . *want* to come with you?"

Roonan ignored her and continued muttering. Then he began to do some strange motions with his hands. Finally, he pricked a finger and let one drop of dark-blue blood land on one of the glowing rocks.

Litney shuddered.

Roonan was trying to carefully carve out two rocks when he turned around suddenly, a look of horror flashing across his face. Litney whirled to look behind her, sure Mala had discovered them, but when she didn't see anything behind her, she turned to face Roonan again. "What? What's wrong?"

"Breath Bandit," he croaked, raising his knife again to cut himself.

"No, stop. Please don't hurt yourself anymore," Litney begged, until it occurred to her there was only one other way to save Roonan. She blurted, "Oh, but then I have to kiss you."

The knife started to cut through the bandage on his arm.

"Stop!" Litney cried. She knew she only had a few more seconds before the Breath Bandit took all of Roonan's breath, so she stood on her tiptoes and kissed the head that looked just like a falcon's. It was a quick one, but she hoped it did the job.

It must have because the fear on Roonan's face subsided, and he started to pull in big deep breaths. "Thank you," he said.

"No, thank you," a voice from behind them murmured. It was Mala's.

* 13 *

"Once again, it's your stupidity that will be *your* undoing," Mala declared as she stared at Litney. In her disguise as a Gadlander, Mala was beautiful—her fur a royal purple, her eyes that same intense green that they had been the last time Litney had met her. Around her shoulders, she wore something that looked like a shawl, and its yellow glimmer was so rich, Litney was sure it had somehow been spun from pure gold.

Mala had continually called Litney stupid the last time they had faced each other in a cave, and it had made her furious. Now, knowing the creature was trying to get a rise out of her, Litney forced herself to be calm before she spoke. Even to her own ears, she sounded strangely powerful and brave when she observed, "Once again, it is your greed that will be *your* undoing."

Mala must have heard the change in Litney's voice, because she shifted her weight uneasily. Perhaps Mala realized she was showing fear, because she stood taller and said, "I see you have the bracelet, which means things are going exactly as I planned. I knew you were listening to us, I knew you would come here when you thought the Breath Bandits and Ignitatus were gone. Too bad for you we were all here, waiting for you to show up."

All here? That meant Mala wasn't the only one she and Roonan were going to need to fight.

"Let's not make it so difficult this time, shall we?" Mala said. "Give me the bracelet."

"No," Litney said simply.

Mala gave a low growl. "I will not have my plans ruined."

"What are yer plans? Why Gad?" Roonan asked, joining the conversation for the first time. "Ye've ruined my land, my home. I deserve to know why."

When her laugh died away, Mala answered, "You deserve nothing. Oh, but look at you. So sad. You've lost an eye, and you're all battered. You poor fool. Why didn't you just give up and join the others of your kind in their mindlessness up top?"

"Because I love my home, and I'm willing to fight for it," Roonan growled. "I'll have ye tell me why ye've destroyed it." With that, Roonan ran toward Mala's neck with both his hands outstretched. Before he could reach her, however, there was a cracking sound as a wave of fire flashed in the cave, catching him directly in the chest. His body curled in on itself and he fell to the ground as the smell of burnt fur filled Litney's nostrils.

Litney was going to rush to help him when he shouted at her, "Stay back!" She didn't move, except to turn and look at the place where the flames had come from. Standing there, she saw a horse-like creature whose entire body seemed to be made of fire. The Ignitatus. And here she was, trapped in a cave with it, Mala, and probably a herd of invisible Breath Bandits. On top of that, now Roonan was hurt on the floor.

Bracelet, she thought to herself, *I know you didn't like what I was wishing for earlier, but I could really use some help right now. Can you put out the Ignitatus?*

"No," a voice said aloud in the cave.

"No what?" Mala wanted to know, glaring at Litney.

"Uh, no, I will not give you the bracelet," she said, hoping Mala wouldn't figure out it was actually the bracelet that had spoken.

Mala seemed ready to pounce on Litney at this declaration, but then she must have thought better of it, because she drawled, "Ignitatus, dear. I think our friend here needs some of your special attention."

The horse-like head nodded, and the red beast with the red eyes began to walk toward Litney. It was hard for her to look directly at it—the fire that was its skin shone as harshly as the sun. But one thing Litney could manage to see was its fiery tail which seemed at least two times as long as a horse's, and it crackled as it swished this way and that as the Ignitatus walked closer.

I wish you would . . . would . . . Litney started to beseech the bracelet, her eyes searching frantically around the cavern for something that could help her. Nothing. Nothing! And the bracelet had grown such an attitude, what was she supposed to wish for?

"I cannot wait for the Ignitatus to burn you," Mala said with a maniacal glee lighting her eyes. "You won't be able to survive his tail for long. One swipe, maybe two, or even three, if you are braver than you look. But do you really want to suffer like that? And if you do manage to live, just think how scarred your pretty little face will be."

The Ignitatus had stopped walking. It turned a little, and its tail flashed closer and closer to her, cracking every time.

"You are not that brave," Mala said, her voice a little frantic when Litney did not answer. "Come on now, give me the bracelet."

Even though she couldn't figure out what to ask the bracelet for, Litney stood her ground. Her mind kept sifting through different possibilities, but it was getting more and more difficult to think as that tail of fire sailed closer and closer to her body.

"You leave me no choice," Mala told her and her gesture told the creature to strike away.

Please take Roonan and me away from here, Litney begged the bracelet in her mind.

"No," came the emphatic reply.

Again, Mala thought it was Litney who had spoken. "No? You don't want to be burned? Then give me the bracelet."

"I will not."

Before Mala had even finished giving a go-ahead nod, the Ignitatus' tail struck Litney for the first time, the fire searing through her jeans and the flesh on her shin. The pain made her crumple to the ground, and her hands grabbed at the wound. What was she going to do? The bracelet was being difficult, this thing was about to cook her piece by piece and Roonan was struggling to get up, but he couldn't. He kept falling back to the sand and clutching at his chest. She bent her head to look at the wound once more, and a drop of wet, salty sweat landed in her eye. Suddenly her crazed mind provided her with a crazy wish, *I wish you would make my sweat so powerful that it would put out any fire the Ignitatus uses on me.*

"Yes," the bracelet said, and Litney could have sworn it sounded amused.

"Yes?" Mala sneered. "Yes, continue to burn you bit by bit? Oh, I will make sure that happens. Unless you give me the bracelet."

"No," Litney replied, standing tall once again. Her only hope was that the bracelet would do what she asked. But was that possible? Could sweat be so powerful it would put out fire? It was both gross and doubtful.

When the tail struck her for the second time, it felt like she was back on the playground, and one of those jump ropes made out of the hard plastic beads had hit her. But there was no burning or smell. A little steam rose in the air, but even her shirt where the tail had hit her was still whole and unharmed.

Mala let out a little shriek, and whether it was from fear or frustration, Litney couldn't tell. "Strike her again!"

The fiery tail snaked through the air again, this time curling itself around her legs. However, as soon as it hit her, it fizzled out and disappeared.

"How are you doing that?" Mala screamed.

Litney raised one eyebrow and shrugged. Yes, the sweat was pouring down her body now, but she didn't care. She reveled in it.

"Hit her again and again and again!"

The Ignitatus complied, unleashing its flaming tail at Litney's body over and over. As she stood stock still, she whispered, "Thank you," to the bracelet.

"Stop!" Mala cried after several minutes of this, her eyes so wide, the whites were showing.

Deciding to go on the offensive, Litney said, "Yes, let's stop this, shall we? Why are you here, Mala? What do you want with the bror and the liquid and the bracelet?"

"I will not tell you," the creature spit out.

"It's obvious I'm a bit more powerful than last time we met, so why don't we talk this out?" Litney bluffed. Or at least she thought she was bluffing.

Mala began to stalk back and forth. Apparently the shawl around her neck must have been bothering her, because she clawed at it and wadded it up before throwing it half way across the cavern from where she stood. "You are not powerful. I am, and I will be even more so." It seemed Mala was growing more and more out of control, because she began to run off at the mouth, unknowingly answering Litney's question as she declared, "I will have the bracelet so I can have unlimited power, bror to hide me so I can do whatever I want wherever I want, and the liquid to help me so I can live forever."

I was right! Litney thought to herself. When she had seen the ledger and that picture of Talmoon, she had thought this had something to do with the fountain of youth, that magic elixir that was said to let people live forever. But it had seemed so far-fetched, she hadn't told Dokken or Asta what she had been thinking. But then why hadn't the tea bags worked for the king? They had worked for her.

"Crush her," Mala whispered, finally getting herself back under control.

The Ignitatus charged and reared. Its red and fiery front hooves came crashing down on Litney, and she was sure she was dead. Fleetingly, she hoped Dokken would make it back home safely.

But when the hooves touched her, they did not burn or sear her flesh. Instead, the hooves turned into water. Then the entire front legs of the creature disappeared in a wet whoosh. Before she could think, Litney grabbed its head in her hands, and the creature trembled for a moment before its head went from fiery red to watery blue. The water splashed to the ground, and what was left of the body of the creature crumbled to the ground. The flames sputtered for a bit on the sand before they flickered and went out. All that remained looked like a tree trunk that had been in a campfire—thick and burnt and charred.

"You . . . you . . . you killed the Ignitatus! But how?" The look in Mala's eyes was akin to what Litney had seen in Talmoon's as he paced back and forth in his cell: unhinged. "It doesn't matter. It doesn't matter! I will have the bracelet still!"

From the way Mala was crouching down, Litney could tell the creature was about to pounce on her. She knew she had only a few seconds to think. It appeared the bracelet had grown a sense of humor, if letting Litney use sweat to defeat the Ignitatus was any indication. What if it would only grant off-the-wall requests, not ones that were obvious or made any sense? So what could she ask it? How could she use it to defeat Mala? It had to be something weird, maybe gross. Her mind went to what kids had thought was funny in third grade. Burping, farting, puking. Puking. That was it!

Mala launched herself into the air, and Litney had just enough time to wish, *I wish Mala would puke, would puke flowers every time she tried to steal the bracelet—for now and forever.* As soon as she had finished thinking her wish, she threw herself to the sand in order to avoid being crushed by Mala's leaping body.

Mala crashed to the sand next to Litney and began making the most horrible sound. It was worse than the sound her cat made when it had a hair ball. Litney realized she was hearing full-fledged puking. And even as she began to grimace at the noise, she turned her head and saw a pile of bright blue flowers pouring out of Mala's mouth and onto the ground beneath her.

"What," Mala began, but had to stop because more flowers were forcing their way out of her mouth, "what have you done to me?"

Litney stood, brushed the sand sticking to her body, and answered, "I used the bracelet to defeat you."

"You haven't defeated m—" Mala couldn't finish her thought, because a bunch of purple flowers flew out of her mouth and even her nose. "You have not! I will get the brace—" and when Mala lunged toward her, a shower of what looked like sunflowers shot out of her mouth.

"Go home, Mala. Leave Gad alone. Leave all the worlds alone. We're finished. Do you hear? I wished that you would puke every time you tried to steal the bracelet—for now and forever. So if you don't like what you are feeling—and I don't see how you could—then leave me and the bracelet alone."

"Never!" Mala vowed, but she did not charge at Litney again. Instead she took a couple of steps backward.

"Now will you answer a question?" Litney asked.

"Never!" Mala repeated.

"I was just curious if you knew I would be sent here. If that was part of your plan. Was it?"

A roar came out of Mala's mouth as she charged once again at the girl. But before she could take her second step, she fell to her knees again and threw up a huge pile of what looked like green hydrangeas.

Litney knew she probably would never get that particular question answered, so she spoke to the bracelet, "Can I wish that you would send her back to her world?"

"Yes," the bracelet murmured, and with that, the vomiting Mala was gone.

Litney rushed over to Roonan and knelt down beside him. "Are you okay?" Gently she turned him over and gasped. There was a thick charred gash that ran like a deep channel from one side of his chest to the other.

"No," Roonan gasped. "I don't think—"

"Hush," Litney interrupted.

"It went too deep," Roonan said.

"Bracelet, can you please save him?"

"No," the bracelet said sadly.

"But he did so much to help Gad. Please."

"No."

All the bravery and courage Litney had felt when she was facing the Ignitatus and Mala disappeared, leaving her afraid, deflated. "But he can't—" Litney's words were cut short, because she had felt a tickle in her chest. Maybe she had to sneeze. She prayed she just had to sneeze. But no, she was sure a Breath Bandit had just crawled inside her lungs.

"Roonan," she said.

He didn't respond.

"Roonan, I think a Breath Bandit is in me. It's beginning to be hard . . . to breathe." He still didn't move, so there was no chance he could kiss her. That left hurting herself. She slapped at her cheek—it was getting harder to breathe. She punched herself in the stomach—she was gasping now. She remembered Roonan cutting himself over the bror. Maybe that's what she needed to do. When she looked toward the glowing rocks, she saw Roonan's knife in the sand. He must have dropped it when Mala startled them.

She began to make her way toward the knife . . . just ten steps. She could make it. How many seconds had gone by? Probably nine, ten. Was she going to make it? Yes.

No. Her eyes began to blur and she collapsed.

14

Dokken's face was close to hers. How did he get there? Why did her lips feel wet? And what was that look in his eyes?

When he saw her eyes had opened, Dokken sat back on his heels and released a shaky breath. "I thought I was too late," he said.

"How did you get here?" Litney whispered, wishing the numbing fog in her head would disappear.

Dokken stood up and started to walk back and forth. "When you left, it hit me what I had just done. How could I let you go out there and face Mala and the other things all by yourself?"

"Roonan was with me," she pointed out.

"Yes, but you're my, my friend and uh," even in the shadowy cave, Litney could see his face reddening, "and uh, I let you down. I was a coward."

"Mala killed you last time, and she said she would do the same thing this time," she reminded him, pushing herself up onto her elbows. She thought about sitting up the whole way, but even this little movement made her head start to swirl.

"That's true," Dokken admitted as he continued pacing, "but I was still a coward. And I knew it. And I hated it. So I decided I'd follow you all, but as soon as I opened the door, as soon as I saw that darkness, I knew I'd never be able to find you. I'd get lost. Part of me thought I should just go out into that darkness, get lost, starve to death. That's what I deserved. You can't imagine how horrible I felt as I closed the door again. I sat on the floor and that was probably the longest and worst hour or two of my life. But then I heard you all talking. I couldn't figure out how, but I could, and then I realized it was the box at Roonan's. I heard what you were planning."

"Really?" This surprised Litney, since she and Roonan had talked while they were inside the bubble that the bracelet had provided. It should have been soundproof.

"I knew you were in some sort of protective shield, but, yeah, I could hear everything you were saying. I heard it all as it was happening. I was almost wild when I figured out the Ignitatus was there. I was sure you were going to die. But then I heard Mala say you had killed it. But I couldn't figure out how did you defeated it. What did you do?" he asked, sitting down on the ground.

"You won't believe me," Litney chuckled. She tried sitting up and found her head was okay with that.

"Try me."

"The bracelet," Litney began, her eyes taking in the piece of jewelry on her wrist, "seems to have grown a little attitude. Everything I asked it to do, it kept saying no."

"You don't mean it actually said no, do you?"

"Yeah, I do. It almost got me into trouble with Mala. I didn't know what to do, because it nixed everything I was saying, but then when the Ignitatus was about to strike me for the second time, some sweat landed in my eye."

"It is awfully hot in here," Dokken agreed, wiping at his forehead.

"So, I thought maybe I should try a weird request. I asked the bracelet to make my sweat so powerful that it would put out the Ignitatus' fire."

"You're kidding," Dokken said.

"Nope. So when it started hitting me with its fiery tail, it couldn't burn me. When it reared and was going to crush me, it turned to water instead. I grabbed its head with my hands to finish it off and—oh no!" she exclaimed. "Roonan. This fog in my head. I forgot until now! How is he? Is he—"

"I didn't think about him," Dokken admitted. "Where is he?"

"Over here. Come on." They found Roonan in a curled-up position, still breathing, but barely.

"Can't the bracelet save him?" Dokken asked, his face white when it saw what the Ignitatus's tail had done to the Gadlander.

"I already asked it if it could, and it said no."

"That's right. I heard that."

Litney wondered how he could have heard that, because it was only seconds later when she had felt the Breath Bandit in her lungs, but she didn't have time to ask about that now. "We've got to help him. There has to be something we can do." Around Roonan's bodies were the piles of flowers Mala had thrown up. "These flowers . . . what if we . . . yes, we need to take some of these flowers and put them in his wound."

"Why in the world would we do that?" Dokken questioned.

"Something is telling me we should. You try to get him to relax and lay on his back. I'll figure out which flowers we should use."

As Dokken worked on coaxing Roonan's body into a straighter position, he watched as Litney walked over to the different piles of flowers. She would smell one, rub it on her hand, and then she would toss it back into the pile. When she got to a pile of blue flowers, she smelled, rubbed, then smelled again.

"This is it," she said, running back to Roonan's side. "These are the ones we want. Gather as many as you can and help me pack them into his wound."

Dokken got up and wandered over to the pile of blue flowers, but he shook his head. "That's crazy. Putting flowers in a wound? What's that gonna do? And, hey, didn't I hear you tell Mala that you asked the bracelet to have her throw up flowers whenever she tried to get the bracelet? That means these have been—ewwwww," he threw the one blue flower he had picked up to the ground and began wiping his hands on his pants.

"Dokken!" Litney shouted. "We don't have time for this. Gather as many blue flowers as you can. Now!"

Since he hadn't expected her to go all military commander on him, he jumped, and then he did as he was told.

She took the blossoms from Dokken's hands and began gently pressing them into the wound. Roonan moaned. Dokken opened his mouth to say something, but Litney's glare made him close it again without speaking.

When the entire burnt channel had been filled with flowers, Litney laid her hands as lightly as she could on top of Roonan's chest. She began to murmur, "I know you said you couldn't save him, bracelet, but I would still like to ask for your help. These flowers, there's something about them. When I smelled them, it was like I was in a cool lake back home. Since Roonan is all burnt, these flowers should soothe him. These flowers have a power in them, too. If you could just help the flowers be even more powerful, I would appreciate it." She didn't say anymore, just kept her fierce eyes on Roonan's face. He moaned again, and then again.

"Litney, are you sure about this?"

"Shhh," she whispered, "the fire is coming out of him. Feel the backs of my hands."

He did, and he had to yank his hand away from hers because it felt as if he had touched a hot stove. "Your hand is burning," he exclaimed.

"I know. Isn't it weird?" she said softly. "Somehow these flowers and my hands are drawing the fire out of him. It's working. I know it." But then big tremors started to run throughout Roonan's body, and Litney thought about pulling her hands away from him. He seemed to be in such pain! But before she had started doing this, he had been maybe ten breaths away from dead, she was sure of it. She decided to see it through.

She was glad she did, because in another minute or two, Roonan's body stopped shaking, his breathing smoothed, and his eyes fluttered open. He blinked several times. "So, I'm not dead, then," he murmured.

Dokken and Litney laughed. "No, ye're not," Dokken mimicked.

"And how about Mala? I saw what ye did with the Ignitatus. Was that the bracelet's doing?"

"Mala is gone, and yes, the bracelet helped me defeat them both."

"Then I am mighty glad ye were here with that bracelet. Ye've saved me and my world."

After Litney asked the bracelet to turn any remaining Breath Bandits into purple mushrooms, the three of them spent the next hour or so explaining everything that had happened to one another. Litney told everything that had happened with Mala and the Ignitatus, and Dokken explained that as soon as he heard Litney say a Breath Bandit had crawled in her, he had rushed outside and found the *sirihiri* rock in that tower they had first touched. He had grabbed hold of it and then had whispered, "Please, take me to the other rock," and magically, it had. He had appeared in the cave, had found Litney on the ground. It was here that he paused in the story, and it was then Litney realized that Dokken had kissed her, but she kept that revelation to herself. She was glad she had been unconscious when it had happened.

Or at least most of her was glad.

"So now what? What about the king?" Litney asked after a while. "He must have gone back up top. How are we going to get up there? And when we do, do you really think he's going to say with a big smile, 'Oh, *you're* right. Let's go back to the way Gad was'?"

"No, I don't," Roonan growled. He was sitting up now.

When Litney looked at him, she thought maybe he was still in pain because of the way he was holding his body, but then it became clear it wasn't pain that he was feeling, it was rage.

"He let that Mala thing destroy our world. He, he, I'm going to kill him." Roonan stood but started to sway dangerously.

"Sit down," Litney ordered, and the big Gadlander grumpily obeyed. "You need to rest a little longer. And you're not going to kill anyone. Yes, I understand what he did to your world, but you don't need his blood on your hands. And do you think that's going to help convince all the others up there that they need to tear everything down and get back to the way Gad was?"

"It'd make me feel better," Roonan growled.

"I understand that, but what's more important? You feeling better for a little bit and then getting thrown in some kind of a cell for the rest of your life or getting Gad back to the way it was?"

He growled again and slammed his huge fist into the sand.

"I take your silence to mean that you see my point?" Litney pressed.

A curt nod was her answer.

"So how do we get the king and everyone else up there to realize what they've done, to realize what they're missing?"

Apparently Dokken had forgotten that Mala had thrown up all the flowers strewn about the cave, because he was going from pile to pile and smelling them. He held one of them up and said, "How 'bout using these?"

"Why would we bring them flowers?" Roonan asked as he glared at the boy.

"Because they healed you, and . . . I don't know. There's something about them. Plus, I remember reading somewhere back home that the sense of smell is the most immediate and powerful sense, at least that we humans have. And since you all love these flowers, it seems like that would be true for you, too. Bring them these flowers and remind them what they have been missing."

"I'm not bringing the king flowers," Roonan muttered. "I'm bringing him pain and—"

"Roonan," Litney warned. "We covered that. No, you're not bringing him pain. You want Gad back. That's the big picture, okay? Let's focus on that. I think Dokken's right about the flowers. Let's gather as many as we can, and then see if we can find our way up top."

WHEN HE FELT STRONG AGAIN, ROONAN led them back to his house. This time, the bracelet's light shone bright around them, and Litney could see how beautiful Gad was. There were grasses and strange trees that didn't grow straight up, but instead bent at right angles, perfect for sitting in. "How are things still growing down here?" she asked Roonan as they walked along. "It's dark. In our world, plants need light to grow."

"I have wondered that meself," Roonan said. "My only guess is that Gad is a very good land. That somehow it has enough . . . something still in its soil to nurture what wants to keep growing here. We have three suns, and the light from them was so beautiful. Maybe the land took in as much as it could and was able to store it somehow."

"I sure hope you can get it back to the way it was," Litney whispered.

"Me, too," Roonan answered as they gathered more flowers from his house and then returned to stand in front of the slide that was right outside the Door. "Bracelet, can you please create steps in this slide so we can climb up?"

The slick slide buckled and heaved and a staircase appeared before them. They climbed and came to stand before the Door that was so tightly shut they couldn't even see the edges of it. Litney asked the bracelet, "Can you help us get through so we can get Gad back to the way it was?"

The Door shimmered for a moment and then disappeared. Harsh light from Gad burned their eyes. Before their eyes could adjust, guards grabbed them and shoved their wrists into something that felt like it was as inescapable as if cement had just hardened around them.

"ISN'T THIS DELIGHTFUL," THE KING ASKED with a wicked light making his eyes shine. "Not only have you defeated that nasty Mala creature for me, but you've also brought me Roonan, my dearest dearest friend."

At this, Roonan lunged toward the king but he didn't get very far. That's because the guards stuck out their legs, tripping him. Since his hands were bound, he couldn't stop himself from hitting the ground hard.

The king chuckled as he lounged in the chair and flicked his fingers toward the thrashing Gadlander. Two guards approached him, pointing their needle guns at his rage-filled face. He must have decided struggling was pointless, because he began to settle down, so they hauled him to his feet. "Oh, Roonan, so earnest. You love Gad dearly, don't you? I'm sure you thought you could come up here and convince me now to turn it all back to the way it was. All that land and sky. But you see, my friend—"

"I—am—not—your—friend," Roonan ground out.

"You see, my friend," the king continued as though there had been no interruption, "I like Gad like this. When Mala first told me to cover up the land and the bror mine somehow, I couldn't imagine doing it. But now, I can't imagine ever living without all this shiny bright light. And, obviously, it was something my people wanted since every single one of them joined me."

"I didn't want it. I didn't join *you*," Roonan argued.

Again, the king ignored him completely. "Yes, this is how Gad will be, because it makes me happy."

The king looked anything but happy, Litney thought to herself. More like deranged. She tried a quick silent wish to the bracelet: can you please turn the king into a turnip with a head so we can try talking some sense into him?

"No," the bracelet said aloud.

"What did *you* say?" the king asked, narrowing his eyes at Litney.

"No, I mean, but the Gad down there is good and beautiful," she managed to get out, thinking the bracelet's attitude was getting old. Taking a deep breath, she continued, "By making it safe and bright and slick, *you've* made it meaningless. You've taken away what made Gad Gad. You took away what made *your* people people. You've made them into expressionless creatures who . . . who aren't even allowed names." This hadn't occurred to Litney until it came out of her mouth. She had never heard the king called anything but the king, and Miss Bootlicker, that wasn't a name, at least not a name like Roonan. "You've made it so that everyone is only called by their role, haven't *you*? Remember, Dokken?" She turned to the boy and reminded him, "Miss Bootlicker thanked the Carriers when we first arrived here. He's taken away all of their names."

"It is easier without names," the king declared. "Who can ever remember names?" He rose from his throne and began pacing back and forth on the dais. "I'm tired of this. I'm tired of *you*. Throw them in a cell!" he commanded.

"No!" Dokken shouted, stepping in front of Litney when two guards began to move toward them. "We gave *you* what *you* wanted. We got rid of Mala and the Ignitatus. You need to let us go. And Talmoon and Pansy."

"Don't you get it? I could care less about you, about any of you. This is my world. My world! So you will join your friends and stay in cells forever for no other reason than because that is what I want. Ah, Miss Bootlicker. Perfect timing, as usual. Please show these three to the places they will be spending the rest of their lives."

Neither Litney nor Dokken had seen Miss Bootlicker enter. She had come from somewhere behind them and now she stood at Litney's side. What was odd was Miss Bootlicker's attention wasn't on the king, it was on Litney.

"What are you staring at?" Litney asked. The way the creature was staring at her, it seemed as if she was about to bend down and eat her.

"Nothing, nothing," Miss Bootlicker whispered.

Litney could have sworn she saw the creature swaying beside her.

"Get them out of here!" the king commanded.

The guards hooked a chain onto each of the cuffs around their wrists and pulled Litney, Dokken and a struggling, howling Roonan from the room.

15

LITNEY'S CURLED BODY HUDDLED in a corner of the room. She had her eyes closed and her hands over her ears. She could block out most of the nauseating dance of light going on around her, but she couldn't stop the screeching noise assaulting her ears. No matter how much she pleaded, the bracelet did nothing to help her block it all out.

She had only been in her cell for a couple of hours and already she could feel herself losing control. No wonder Talmoon's eyes had looked as they did . . . she wondered if he had gone crazy yet. She didn't think it would take her long to get there.

Litney tried readjusting her hands to cover her ears better. When the noise stopped abruptly, she didn't pull her hands away from her ears. What if she had just found the exact way to plug her ears so that no noise could sneak in? Did she dare pull her hands away, because what if the noise was still going on and she couldn't find this exact position again?

Someone tapped her shoulder. Cracking open one eye, she looked up. It was Miss Bootlicker, and she was tugging on Litney's arm to try and get the girl to stand up.

Litney stood and heard, "Fee hap poop flurry." Litney shook her head.

Miss Bootlicker reached up and pried the girl's hands away from her ears. When her ears were free, Miss Bootlicker repeated what she had said, this time making much more sense, "We have to hurry." Without another word, the Gadlander turned and climbed the stairs up out of the cell.

Litney hesitated. Was she being taken to some new and even more horrifying place? Did she dare to follow Miss Bootlikcer? Did she dare not to?

Something in her gut told her it would be wise to do what Miss Bootlicker said, so Litney followed her. The two of them soon arrived at

Dokken's cell. Scrunched in the corner just like she had been, it took awhile for Dokken to be convinced that he should let his hands be pulled from his ears.

"Follow me," Miss Bootlicker urged.

Dokken's face questioned Litney. Since she had no answers, all she could do was shrug.

As the two of them trailed behind Miss Bootlicker, Litney wondered where she was taking them.

Up was the only answer she had at the moment. The three of them had gone into what could only be described as the back region of Gad. Like the backstage of a theater, it was shadowy and there were staircases they climbed, catwalks they crossed, and ladders they scaled. Litney couldn't imagine where they were going. In the dim light, she saw Miss Bootlicker hold up her hand. They stopped. Then Miss Bootlicker put her hand flat over her mouth. Litney guessed that meant they should be quiet. Finally, the Gadlander pointed over what appeared to be an edge. Dokken and Litney approached it and peered over. Below them they saw a brightly lit room that would have made them gasp if Miss Bootlicker hadn't warned them to be quiet. This was the only room either of them had seen in this above-Gad world that didn't have glowing walls. The walls in this room were painted a soothing tan color, and the floor seemed to have actual grass growing on it. In the middle of the room there was a hut, and while she hadn't seen anything clearly because of the dark, Litney guessed this hut was just like Roonan's.

A door to the room opened, and in walked the king with his black dead eyes. He must have been angry or upset about something, because the first thing he did was to stalk over to a flower growing alongside the hut and rip it out of the ground with his big hand. As soon as he whipped it across the room, he must have regretted the action, for he dashed over to the flower, picking it up and cradling it. He put the blossom to his nose and inhaled deeply. Then he began talking to the flower. "I don't know what to do. That nasty creature is dead, and so I have my world back. But I heard that creature muttering about a liquid that would help her live forever. I never knew what the liquid was, why it mattered. I just did what the creature told me. I built that platform to connect the portals. I found the man named Gunner, promised him big things, told him I'd get rid of his brother and give him back the girl. But the liquid didn't work. Those kids lied to me. Lied to me! I'll kill them for it. Kill them! What's that?" the king asked, putting the flower to the side of his head, as if it were speaking tho him. "Maybe they didn't know what they were doing? You think I should ask Talmoon? But I don't want to talk to Talmoon," the king pouted. "I don't like him. He's too, too steady and when he and that woman look at each other, I want to scream."

The king began storming around the room in a frenzied circle. "I don't want to talk to him!" he shouted at the flower in his hand. "You can't make me!"

Without warning, the king fell to his knees. He buried his face in the grass, and Litney and Dokken could hear him inhaling deeply. "Fine!" the king shouted, his face turned upward. It almost seemed as if he had been shouting directly at the three of them. Litney and Dokken ducked behind the ledge, only to peek back over it when they heard the king knocking three times on the door. It opened, and he left the room.

Miss Bootlicker led them away from the edge, down several ladders, along two halls, down three staircases and pulled them into yet another brightly lit room. The only thing in this one was what looked like a very hard bed. There were no covers, no squishy mattress, only a glass box projecting covers and pillows. "This is my bedroom," she explained. "You may talk now. I'm certain you have questions."

That was an understatement, Litney thought as so many questions stampeded through her brain that she didn't even have time to think how horrible a bedroom this would be to have. "Why did you get us out of our cells?"

"So you could witness that," the Gadlander replied coolly.

"But why would you want us to see that?" Dokken asked. "To let us know that your king's crazy and that we shouldn't do anything to make him angry?"

"No, because you needed to see that all is not lost," Miss Bootlicker replied, her hands clasped properly in front of her. "Even though he won't admit it, the king misses the old Gad. He needs the old Gad."

"But why would you help us? What would make you betray your king?" Litney wanted to know.

There was a pause. "That," the Gadlander said simply, pointing at Litney's hair.

"What are you pointing at?" Dokken asked. He saw Litney, that was all.

"She has a flower in her hair. When I came to stand next to you in the throne room, I got a whiff of it. I have not smelled a Falling Light flower in who knows how long, but as soon as I caught its scent, it made me go tumbling all the way back to when I was a child. My mother, brother, and I would go out into the fields and pick flowers. My brother did what he was told: he collected eight green flowers, three orange ones, ten black ones. I, however, ignored every other flower in the fields. I would only pick Falling Lights. My mother used to get so angry with me, but no matter what punishment she threatened me with, I would still only gather those."

"Would you like to smell it? Eat it?" Litney asked, pulling the flower from her hair, thinking it was a good thing she had decided to be silly and put one behind her ear as they had been gathering flowers to bring up to the king. Things had happened so quickly, they hadn't had the chance to offer the blossoms to the king, but based off of what they had just seen him doing in his room, as well as Miss Bootlicker's reaction, Litney wished they had.

"Oh," Miss Bootlicker burbled, wringing her hands. "I couldn't."

"You can and you should. Here. Enjoy."

With her big hand, the Gadlander took the flower from Litney and put her nose right in the blossom. She inhaled, pulling its fragrance into her nose, into her very soul it seemed. Her eyes rolled closed. She opened her mouth and took the blossom in slowly. She must have been so overtaken by taste and memory that she melted to the floor. "Oh, my," was all she could utter.

"We had the same reaction," Dokken told her. "Oh, no, well, we didn't cry. Litney, she's crying. Make her stop. Litney. She's crying."

"Are you okay?" Litney asked, glaring at Dokken. Then she pulled out the yellow purse and said, "I have a whole bunch of flowers in here if you would like more. We were going to offer them to the king. We wanted to try to remind him of what he had given up."

"I had forgotten what we gave up," Miss Bootlicker admitted, tears as big as grapes falling out of her eyes. "I gave up taste and joy and delight. And my name. Can you imagine? I gave up my name. I let myself be called Miss Bootlicker."

"What is your name?" Litney asked gently as she bent down to squat beside the Gadlander.

"Sakrista," the Gadlander whispered, almost as if she was saying something naughty.

"Sakrista," Litney repeated, sticking out her right hand. "You scared the bejeebers out of me as Miss Bootlicker. I like you much better like this. I'm glad you remembered what you had forgotten."

"What am I supposed to do?" Sakrista asked, gazing at Litney's outstretched hand.

"Put your huge Gadlander hand in mine. Then we shake. It's our way of saying, 'Nice to meet you.'"

Sakrista put her hand in Litney's and said, "Nice to meet you?"

"Nice to meet you," Litney declared, standing and helping Sakrista do the same.

Dokken waved. "Yeah. Cool. Nice to meet you. Much better. But the thing is, now what do we do? I mean, whose side are you on? Litney and I need to help Talmoon and Pansy. Plus, we'd like to help Roonan get Gad back to the way it was."

"I want that as well. Tell me what to do. What can I do to help?"

Litney, ready to forge ahead and brainstorm on what to do next, paused when she saw Dokken's face. "What's wrong?"

"Nothing," Dokken said, not looking at her or Sakrista.

Litney knew they should be moving on with whatever plan they could figure out, but Dokken, clearly upset, wasn't talking. She stomped her foot. "We don't have time for this. Tell me what's wrong. Now."

He gave her a fierce look. "How do we know she won't betray us? You saw the king. Now that he's heard what the magic liquid does, maybe he wants us to trust her so we will help figure out what the magic liquid is. How do we know?"

"You can't," Sakrista admitted. "But look. I know things. Things that can help you."

"Like what?" Dokken eyed her.

"Like Roonan and the king were best friends when we were young.

"If they were the best of friends, how could the king act like that toward Roonan?" Dokken asked. " How could he mock him like that and then throw him in one of those horrible cells?"

"Because people always liked and respected Roonan more. Whenever decisions had to be made, even like what kind of game we were going to play in a field when we were kids, everyone always looked to Roonan. The king tried to hide how much that annoyed him, but I could always tell. And when the king pulled out the paper with the sun on it—"

"Uh, what?" Litney asked.

"That's how we decide who's king. All who are of eligible age gather in the square and everyone pulls a paper from a basket. The one who pulls the paper with the sun on it gets to be king or queen. All of us hoped Roonan would pull the sun, and the king knew that, so when he pulled it—"

"He felt like he didn't deserve to be king? Like no one wanted him?"

"Exactly," Sakrista said. "I'm afraid it did something to him."

Litney thought for a moment, then asked, "Was it the king who decided to build all of this up over Gad?"

Sakrista nodded.

"Why?"

"The king felt like he needed to do something, anything, to get the people to believe he could be a great leader. He tried all sorts of things—like getting rid of money, handing out cakes every Friday afternoon, but then one day, a Gadlander I had never seen before showed up and met with the king. Within a week, the king decided to build a platform on stilts that stood about fifty feet high. On this platform, he put a tall and shiny building. It sparkled in our three suns, and Gadlanders would gather around and stand on the ground, oooohing and ahhhing at the beautiful new building. They started to say he was the greatest king Gad had ever had, and so the king built another platform and another building. This one had a staircase that mechanically moved up while a different one moved down. Gadlanders would stand in line all day just to ride the stairs. There was nothing at the top, nothing at the bottom. Nothing in the building at all, except stairs that moved. And then the king built another platform and another. It wasn't until almost a quarter of Gad had been covered by platforms that some Gadlanders began to worry. And then some Gadlanders began to speak out, saying this was wrong. That Gad was being destroyed. But by this time, the king was loved by the people, and the king wasn't about to let anyone get in the way of that."

"So what did he do?" Litney asked.

"He captured as many as he could and put them in cells, and he kept on building."

"But he didn't catch all of them," Dokken pointed out. "Like Roonan."

"No, he could never catch Roonan, no matter how hard he tried."

"You seem awfully close to the king," Dokken observed, narrowing his eyes. "So why are you betraying him?"

"Dokken," Litney hissed. "That isn't nice."

"No," Sakrista said, holding up her hand. "He has every right to ask that. Actually, I don't think that I am betraying him. You saw him in his room. He still holds onto Gad, the real Gad."

"So why didn't he get rid all of this?" Litney asked, gesturing to the harsh electric light around her.

"Because that Gadlander wouldn't let him. Because he thought everyone would go back to wishing Roonan had become king. That fear, it began to eat away at him. It did something to his mind. The king hasn't been well for a while," Sakrista murmured.

A question occured to Litney. "How long has Gad been like this?"

"About ten years," Sakrista replied.

Litney's brow furrowed and Dokken asked her what was wrong. "I don't see how that's possible. When I talked to Mala, I got the feeling that she wanted me to come here, that she helped to make that happen. But I only met her for the first time a couple of months ago."

Sakrista offered, "I have heard that time does funny things. Maybe our years happen at a different rate than yours do."

Litney flashed back to her first adventure and the argument she'd had with the heron, Grufwin. He had said time was different for the animals in his world, and maybe the same thing held true here. At least, that was the only explanation she could think of. She shrugged, "You are probably right."

"So what are we going to do now?" Sakrista asked.

"We need to help Talmoon and Pansy," Litney said.

"And Roonan and Gad," Dokken added. "But how can we do all that?"

"Let's go down to the throne room and see if we can't figure out what to do," Sakrista told them. They followed her back through the maze of staircases and catwalks and came to a stop outside the door behind the throne.

Even though the throne had a high back, which meant there was little possibility of detection, Sakrista opened the door only as wide as two of Litney's fingers put together. That meant the voices in the throne room had barely any room to fit through and reach them. Litney elbowed Dokken in the stomach because his chin was digging into her back as he leaned over her to try and get his ear closer to the small opening.

"You will give it to me!" the king screeched so loudly that they had no trouble hearing him.

Talmoon kept his voice quiet and low, so his response was inaudible.

"You will tell me," the king's voice rang clearly. "Bring her here."

"No!" they heard Talmoon shout. "Leave her out of this!"

This time, the three of them couldn't hear what the king said, but they thought they could hear sounds of struggle.

"Let her go!" Talmoon roared.

This was followed by a definite thud.

Litney looked at Sakrista, who nodded. It was time. They threw the door open and dashed around the throne.

"Stop!" Sakrista called out to the inhabitants of the room.

If it hadn't been so serious, it would have been laughable—it was like everyone was suddenly trapped in a photograph. There was the king, standing dumbly on the dais, staring at Sakrista. There were the two guards, frozen in the act of pressing their sharp needles into Talmoon's back as he lay sprawled on the floor. There was Pansy caught mid-kick as she had been trying to pry herself free by flinging her body this way and that. Pansy broke the spell first as her feet succumbed to gravity and fell back to the ground. The two guards hauled Talmoon to his feet, a little trickle of blood traveling from his temple to his jaw.

Sakrista spoke. "Enough of this. It's gone too far."

The king stared at her for a moment with his flat black eyes, then he straightened himself, put his hands on his stomach and pronounced, "Miss Bootlicker, you are out of line. And more than that, you have betrayed me. You took these two from their cells. You—"

She interrupted him. "That's not my name."

"Don't you dare," the king whispered. He cleared his throat and resumed, "You have betrayed—"

"I'm not Miss Bootlicker," she interrupted him again. "How could you have ever called me that? Me. Sakrista. Your sister."

"What?" Litney and Dokken demanded at the same time, while the king cried out, "Do not speak!"

"You're his sister?" Dokken asked, his mouth hanging open like a cave.

"Yes, and not just his sister. His twin."

The king put his hands over his ears. "Stop. Stop talking. You must stop talking. I command you to stop."

"Do you remember your name? Do you remember how it came from Father and Grandfather? Tropet and Zitchka?"

"Stop! I said stop!"

"Petchka. You are Petchka. You need to remember that. You pulled out the paper with the sun on it, you became king. You—"

"Shut up!" the king yelled.

"No," Sakrista said in a firm but kind voice. "I will not. You need to hear this. You need to remember. You need to see what you have done. And I think Roonan needs to be here."

The king sank to the floor.

Sakrista nodded to a guard, who hesitated, but then left the room. Then she continued. "You changed. You lost yourself somehow, and instead of fighting for you, I did what you asked of me. And I'm sorry I did. I changed my name, I changed the way I behaved. But mostly I just watched what you did to Gad, and I did nothing. I decided to believe that we needed these lights and no darkness. That we needed everything simple and bright and clean. I think I decided to believe that because I wasn't happy. Roonan told me he wanted to be with someone else, not me."

She loved Roonan? Dokken mouthed to Litney who shrugged as Sakrista continued, "Do you remember the old Gad? It was a Falling Light flower that Litney wore in her hair that helped me remember. Remember how I would never pick anything else?"

The king began to rock back and forth, and when he spoke, his voice was child-like, small and high. "Oh, Mother used to get so mad at you. She used to threaten to shave off all of your fur. But you loved those flowers." The king stopped rocking. Then he repeated, "You loved those flowers."

"I *love* those flowers," Sakrista corrected. "And so do you. I've seen your room."

The king's terrified eyes found his sister's, and he looked like he had been caught stealing cookies. "How did you know?"

"I made it my job to know everything you've done, just like I made it my job to ensure you were able to destroy Gad."

"It's hard to decide who I hate more," Roonan said, his voice so hard that all the lilt was gone from it. He had just entered the room and heard

Sakrista's admission. "Yer brother who devastated, and I mean *devastated* our world, or ye who let it happen. Ye went along with all his whims. Ye let yer brother destroy our world! How could ye do that?" Roonan's good eye stared hard at Sakrista. She held his gaze for a moment, then had to look away.

When Dokken realized Roonan hadn't been in the room to hear why, he explained, "Sakrista said she did it because you didn't—"

"Perhaps we shouldn't be doing this in front of an audience," Sakrista interrupted. She gestured toward the door behind the throne where she and Roonan would have more privacy.

"No," Roonan shook his head. "No. Ye need to answer for yerself. Publicly. Ye let this happen. Just a glance and I can see he isn't well," he gestured toward the king who had gone back to rocking, a frightening blank look on his face, "so it is ye I blame. Ye should be punished. We should lock ye in one of those cells. Ask Talmoon or Pansy here what they think of what ye did to them. Or Litney or Dokken. Or me. Do ye see me? Do ye see what happened to—"

Sakrista's leap onto Roonan was blink-of-the-eye fast. He was so caught off guard that he tumbled onto his back with the weight of her. He recovered quickly, though, and tossed her off him as if she were a sheet and he was climbing out of bed. When the two of them collided again, a sickening thunk echoed through the room.

"We have to stop them," Litney cried, but one of the guards stopped her. He said, "I've known these two all my life. This has been years in the making. They need to finish this."

"But what if they hurt each other?" Dokken asked, disturbed as well by the fighting and roaring coming from the two of them.

"I doubt that'll happen," the guard answered, "but if it must, it must."

"How could ye?" Roonan demanded as he threw himself on top of Sakrista, pinning both of her arms to the ground.

Sakrista twisted and bucked, trying to gain her freedom.

"Tell me!"

"Because you chose her!" Sakrista shouted, tears filling her eyes. "After that, I didn't care about anything anymore. I didn't care what happened to Gad. I was *glad* when it disappeared, when *you* disappeared." Her body went slack, and she turned her head to the side and closed her eyes, sobbing.

"Sakrista," Roonan said, his voice softening once again so that it was at full lilt.

"Don't." A big tear squeezed out of the corner of her eye. "Don't you dare say my name like that. Just get off of me. Please."

Roonan hesitated for a moment, then climbed off and offered her a hand.

She ignored it and stood by herself. Looking at her brother, who was now curled up like a pill bug on the floor, she said, "Roonan, you are king. Or you are if you want to be. I would appreciate it if you could find someone to help my brother. I wish you luck. I really do."

Roonan grabbed Sakrista's arm as she turned to leave. "Where do you think yer going?"

"To a cell. You were right. That's where I belong."

"Knock it off," Roonan growled. "I was overreacting. Yer brother doesn't deserve to be punished, and neither do ye. I knew I was hurting ye. So if ye have to be punished, so do I."

"You didn't sit by and let Gad be destroyed," she whispered, not raising her eyes. "It was so beautiful. How could I do that?"

Roonan hesitated, then hung his head. He admitted, "When yer brother pulled out that sun, I was so angry, I wanted to kill someone. But I couldn't do that, so I decided to hurt someone as badly as I could instead."

As the two of them stared at each other, the guard whispered to Litney and Dokken, "It was she that he hurt."

"Yeah, we figured that out for ourselves," Dokken said wryly.

Finally, Sakrista asked, "Was there ever someone else?"

Roonan's eye danced a little. "No."

"You, *you*, *you*—" Sakrista's arm was cocked as if she were going to haul off and punch Roonan, but before she could do so, Roonan grabbed her and bushed his mouth lightly along hers.

The stunned silence lasted only until Pansy began to applaud wildly and Litney shouted, "Woo hoo!"

Even Talmoon smiled as he looked at the kissing couple.

But it was Dokken who said, "Can we please go home now?"

⁕ 16 ⁕

TALMOON'S EYES STILL LOOKED HAUNTED as Litney and Dokken came to stand beside him and Pansy on the lift that would send them home. "You saved us," Pansy said simply.

Dokken, uncomfortable with the praise, stammered, "We, we didn't really have a choice. His brother would have killed us."

"Perhaps," Talmoon said, "but I have a feeling when we find out all that's happened, we'll discover that you two are quite amazing."

At these kind words from the huge man, Litney joined Dokken in blushing.

"Are ye all ready?" Roonan asked as he walked up. Sakrista stood beside him. Close beside him.

"I think so," Talmoon said.

"I'm sorry about all that happened," Sakrista said.

Pansy shook her head, as if to say, "It's okay," but Talmoon answered, "You did a really bad thing. No, Pansy, it needs to be said. She did. But," he took Sakrista's hand in his own, "it takes a strong person to admit they have done something wrong, and an even stronger one to do something about it. I hope you can get Gad back to the way it was soon."

"Maybe you'll come and visit?" Sakrista asked.

With a chuckle, Talmoon shook his head. "No offense, but I don't think I ever want to come back here. I'm not going to be leaving my wide open, naturally lit fields for a very long time."

Sakrista smiled and said, "I understand. Be well."

"You, too," Talmoon said in his deep voice, nodding to both Sakrista and Roonan. The floor they were standing on began to rise, and the four humans waved at the group of Gadlanders who had congregated to watch them go. In the background, teams of workers were already beginning to dismantle the structures built over their beautiful world.

Luckily, Talmoon was the first to arrive back at the well, so he could grab onto the side with one of his big strong hands. Pansy clung to his other hand, Dokken clung to hers and Litney, dangling at the bottom of the chain, wondered what would happen if they all slipped back down. Would the bottom of the well be glad to drown them in one big wet pile or would they go all the cold way back to Gad?

It appeared they wouldn't be climbing out of the well anytime soon, though either, because Gunner leaned over the edge and demanded of his brother, "What are you doing back here?"

"Nice to see you, too," Talmoon ground out, doing his best to pull four bodies out of the well with the strength of only one of his arms.

"Need some help?" Gunner said with a trace of sneer in his voice.

"No."

"Yes, we do," Pansy corrected her husband. "Please help us, Gunner."

"Knock it off!" Gunner bellowed, and it was then Litney realized Current, out of their view, had starting barking and whining like mad. Gunner grabbed Talmoon's forearm with his two hands and began to pull. There was much bumping and scarping and barking that accompanied the slow climb, but finally, all four of them were free of the well.

There were two things Litney couldn't help noticing. The first was Gunner bending over and picking up the gun he had laid on the ground. The second was Current racing in circles around the entire group and alternating between sharp barking and that weird chewy growling.

"Oh, Current, it is good to see you, too," Pansy said, trying to pet the dog. But the dog was so wired, he couldn't stop moving.

"Are you angry I didn't stop the men?" Current asked, ears down and tail between his legs as he trotted by Pansy. "I didn't smell them."

"No," Pansy said with a laugh. "My, no. I have a feeling I know why you couldn't smell them."

"Why?" the dog asked, and Litney swore he was trembling.

Pansy turned to look at Litney and Dokken. "Did you notice what they smelled like?"

The two kids searched their memories, but couldn't locate a smell to associate with the Gadlanders, so they shook their heads.

"When those two creatures were holding me in the throne room, I thought I smelled grass. But obviously there wasn't any grass around, and that's when I realized it was the creatures that smelled like grass. That's why you couldn't smell them, Current, and you couldn't have stopped them. They were not about to be stopped." Her eyes found Gunner.

Gunner, who had been staring at her, turned away and kicked at the dirt.

As she looked from Gunner to Talmoon to Pansy, Litney thought the silence that followed had the tension of a tornado about to hit.

It was Talmoon's deep voice that started it all. "I deserve some answers. Why did you do it? What do you want, Gunner?"

Gunner wasn't going to beat around the bush. He started right in. "Nothing. Everything. I want *her.*" He nodded in Pansy's direction. "I want to go back in time. I'm sick of time. And if I went back, then I could go all the way back and maybe some of it would make sense."

"*You're* not making any sense," Talmoon muttered.

Pansy shot him a look and then asked in a voice that was soft and bright as the moon, "What would make sense?"

Hearing her voice must have done something to Gunner, because he yelled, "Don't you speak to me like that, like you could care about me. You couldn't. You didn't. You wouldn't. But it's not even that. Fine. I get it. She loved you. You loved him," he said, pointing first at Pansy and then Talmoon. "But she didn't love me."

"I couldn't love you both like that," Pansy whispered.

"No, not you," Gunner barked. "Ma."

Liteny watched Talmoon, and it seemed as if all he wanted to do was walk over and throttle his younger brother. She could see Talmoon's jaw twitching and it made her think he was working awfully hard to calm himself. When he spoke, his voice was polite. "What are you talking about?"

"Remember that Christmas when you were fourteen, and I was twelve? Remember?"

"No."

This seemed to inflame Gunner even more because he cocked his gun and fired off a shot into the air.

Everyone jumped. Talmoon hurried to say, "Look, Gunner, I really don't remember specifically. But tell me about it. What happened?"

"You made Ma a teapot, and she loved it." He said this as if it should explain everything. When no one said anything, he continued, "She used it every day." Again, he was met with silence. Finally, Gunner finished with a shout. "I painted her a picture of a tree that year! Gave it to her right after you gave her your present. Do you know what she said?"

It seemed like Talmoon didn't want to answer, but he had to say something, so he said quietly, "No, I'm sorry. I can't recall."

"She said, 'No tree I've ever seen is this color. Why in the world would you choose that color?' Then she put the painting in the coat closet, and I never saw it again."

"That was years ago!" This time, it was Talmoon's turn to shout. "Heaven almighty. You're still holding onto that?"

"She loved you best," Gunner countered.

"And who got every single one of Pa's tools? Huh? You, you knucklehead. I sure coulda used some of those in all these years. Heck, you've seen this place. I still could use 'em."

"You could buy 'em and you know it," Gunner growled.

"That's not the point. The point is I didn't get those tools, and you did. But I sure as heck didn't aid and abet in your kidnapping because Pa gave you all his tools!"

"But you see, it didn't stop. It never stopped. Ma loved you, the Indians loved you, then she loved you," Gunner pointed at Pansy. "You got everything. You got the *stuff*."

Litney figured they were talking about the fountain of youth elixir. Before she had a chance to wonder what produced it, Talmoon declared, "I shared it with you. You know I shared it with you. Every year, I ship you a case."

"Yeah, but you didn't *want* to give it to me. You only did because I threatened to tell. And you wouldn't ever tell me how you made it," Gunner griped.

"Which is why we're all here in this crazy situation." Talmoon took a step toward his brother. "Put the gun down. We need to settle this."

Litney had thought that Talmoon's shouting would be the most frightening thing, but this quiet voice he was using right now made the hairs on her neck stand up.

"No."

"What are you, chicken?"

Gunner's eyes narrowed. "That isn't going to work. I'm sick of you being in charge. I'm keeping this gun so there is no doubt who's in charge."

"Put it down. This gets finished. Now."

"No."

"Then you're just going to have to shoot me and live with the fact that you took the coward's way out. That, once again, you had to cheat to beat me."

Gunner arched back and bellowed at the sky. When his eyes came to rest on his brother again, he shouted, "Fine." He set his gun on the ground, out of the way, but certainly close enough to make a dash for it if things got out of hand. Then he faced his brother, and the two big men began to circle. Litney thought about Sakrista and Roonan fighting each other, and somehow she doubted Talmoon and Gunner would end this all by kissing.

"Talmoon," Pansy pleaded, "Don't do this."

"I have to," Talmoon ground out. "I'm sick of this. I'm sick of him. All these years. All these years!" and as soon as that last word had been uttered, Talmoon lunged at his brother. Gunner, not about to be taken off guard, did the same. The two of them smashed together, and the sound was as sickening as it had been when the two Gadlanders had hit. Each of them grabbed at the other man's shoulders and tried to knock him to the ground. While Talmoon was the larger of the two men, Gunner must have been stronger—or at least angrier—because he managed to throw his brother to the ground. He jumped on top of Talmoon and cocked his arm for a punch. Before he could connect with his brother's face, though, Gunner found himself being flipped on his back. Talmoon had swung up a leg, landed it on his brother's chest and slammed him backward.

This time it was Talmoon who climbed on top, pinning his brother's arms under both of his knees. When Talmoon stood up on his knees, all of his torso's weight was on Gunner's arms, so no matter how hard the younger man struggled, he couldn't get free. Talmoon began flicking his brother's nose. "How do you like that, little brother, huh?"

Those watching the fight could see the rage as it sluiced through Gunner's body, and his roar rent the air. Talmoon must have realized he'd pushed his brother too far, because his eyes widened right before he found himself flying backward through the air. He landed right in front of the door to the house, smacking his head on the front step. Before Talmoon could even let out a moan, Gunner was on him, grabbing his neck and starting to squeeze.

Talmoon struggled, slapping at his brother's face, but there was nothing he could do to escape his brother's crushing grip.

Litney was not about to let Gunner kill his brother. She knew there was no way she could physically compete with the two men, but she had her own power. "Please help me burn Gunner's back side," she asked the bracelet. To her surprise, this time the bracelet didn't answer her, it just shot a beam out from the stone and onto Gunner's pants. Smoke began to rise. Before long, Gunner released the grip he had on his brother's neck and twisted around to see what was burning him.

Litney stopped the bracelet's light before he could see that it was coming from her, then caught Pansy mouthing, *Thank you*, to her.

Talmoon didn't know what had made his brother stop strangling him, but he took advantage of the moment and scrambled out from under his brother's weight. He stood and shook his head, trying to get air into his lungs.

Disoriented as he was by what was happening, Gunner was not about to let his brother escape. He launched himself at Talmoon, who was now standing in the doorway of the house. The two of them crashed through the door and slammed into one of the counters. Actually, they slammed into the counter where Litney had left the teapot sitting, the one in which she had brewed the tea bags.

The teapot, knocked off balance, began to spin and sway. "Let go!" Talmoon begged his brother, who once again had him round the neck.

"Never!" his brother retorted.

"No, really, let me go!" but it was too late. The teapot had reached the point of no return. It toppled off the counter and onto the floor, landing hard and shattering.

"Let go, you fool!" Talmoon managed to free one hand and land a hook on his brother's jaw just as Pansy reached the doorway and saw the pile of pottery on the floor. It was difficult to know if it was Talmoon's punch or Pansy's gasp that made Gunner release his hold. Whatever it was, the three of them stood in the kitchen, Talmoon and Pansy staring at the teapot, Gunner staring at his brother and sister-in-law.

"What?" Gunner asked. "What's wrong with you two?"

It was Litney, peeking over Pansy's shoulder, who answered. "Oh . . . it was the *teapot* that was the fountain of youth."

Pansy, with a look that seemed filled with both sadness and relief, turned and looked at her. "How do you know?"

"A bunch of things. Mala, the creature I told you about before we left Gad, let it slip that the magical liquid she was after would let her live forever. But even before that I guessed that you all had some sort of youth elixir. It was the ledger with the handwriting that didn't change, the picture of Talmoon and the Native American. And this teapot," she said, pointing to the pile of shards on the floor. "It looked familiar when I used it, but I didn't know why. It was the one in the photo that Talmoon was holding, wasn't it?

All along I thought it was the tea bags, because of how the tea changed me. But when they didn't work for the king, I figured it had to be something else. I never would have guessed it was the teapot."

Gunner, whose face had gone from angry red shades of rage to the white paleness of shock, fell to his knees. "No," he whispered, trying to fit the pieces of the teapot back together. As he dug through the pile of remains, his fingers were soon covered in a green muck-like substance. The tea bags Litney had left in there must have disintegrated since they had been sitting in the water so long, and the leftover tea had turned to sludge. He wiped his hands off on his pants and moaned, "It can't be." He looked up at his brother, his hands lifted up as if he was begging Talmoon to disagree. When Talmoon didn't say anything, Gunner asked, "What does this mean?"

"That it's over."

"You mean . . ."

"Yes, that's exactly what I mean."

Dokken, who hadn't been able to hear everything, asked, "What does what mean?"

"They broke the teapot, and that means they won't live forever anymore," Litney whispered over her shoulder.

Gunner, who was obviously working himself up into a rage again, was silenced by Pansy, who put her hand on his shoulder and said, "It's how it ought to be. We've pushed this too far. It's best. It really is best. Now we can move on because there's an end we know we will be facing." She reached out and touched Gunner's shoulder. "Now your choices of how you live matter. You don't have forever to figure it out. You only have now. So you have to decide if you're going to stay this angry for whatever time you have left."

Gunner hung his head. "It wasn't fair, how she loved his stuff best."

"No, it wasn't fair," Pansy whispered. "But it's time to let that go."

"I don't know if I can." With that, Gunner stood and shouldered his way out the door.

Talmoon went over to the corner and grabbed a broom. He started to sweep up the remains of the teapot.

"What are you doing?" his wife demanded.

"I'm cleaning up the mess we made."

"You'd better clean up the mess you helped make," she retorted.

"I am!" he spat back.

"Not that one, you idiot. That one!" She pointed out the door to his brother who was growing smaller and smaller the further he walked away from the farm, his gun hanging by his side.

"I didn't make that mess. He did. How in the world can you hold me responsible for any of this?"

"You sat on his chest and flicked his nose," Pansy pointed out.

"What does that have to do with anything?" Talmoon asked, and while his voice was defiant, he began to shift uncomfortably from side to side.

"You were always the big brother who was better at everything. He tried to live up to you, and he couldn't."

"That's not my fault!" Talmoon bellowed.

"Isn't it?" Pansy asked. "Look, would it kill you to go after him and say you're sorry—"

"Say I'm sorry?" Talmoon sputtered. "He's the one who had me kidnapped and tortured"

"I know, love," his wife conceded, her eyes soft. "But there's some really old hurt there. Can't you see what you can do to try and fix it?"

Litney and Dokken backed out of the house, sure that Talmoon would soon turn his rage on someone, and even though Pansy was frustrating him, it wasn't likely to be turned on her. They had barely made it out the door when Talmoon's huge frame came crashing past them. "I can't believe her. She doesn't know what I went through, and she wants me to go after that imbecile and apologize," Talmoon muttered as he stalked off toward his brother.

"Well," Pansy said, stepping outside as she tied an apron around her slim waist. "Are you two hungry? And you, Current," she said, noticing the dog behind them. "Goodness, no one was here to feed you. I'll bet you're starving."

"Yes, ma'am, I am," Current said.

Pansy bent down and stroked the dog's head. Litney couldn't believe it: the dog's vibrating body stilled, and he closed his eyes in what seemed to be deep relaxation and pleasure. Pansy started to scratch Current's back left flank, and the dog started to moan, lifting his back leg and kicking at the air.

"I missed you," he murmured.

"I missed you, too, boy." Pansy gave him one last scratch under his chin, and then she rose. Everyone followed her inside to help make some food, but before long, they heard a shuffling outside. "Talmoon and Gunner must be back," Dokken said, going to the door. "Oh, it's you."

Pansy walked over to the door and then let out a shocked cry of alarm.

"It's okay, Pansy. It's okay," Litney said when she saw Asta retreating from the door into the yard. "She's with us. We know her." To prove that she spoke the truth, Litney walked over to Asta and put her hand on the bear's head. "See?"

"Oh, my, you scared me," Pansy said with a laugh, putting her hand to her heart. "What a way to greet Litney's and Dokken's friend. But a bear! You must forgive me."

"Of course," Asta said. "If I were a human, I would be frightened if I saw a bear in my yard. It's only natural."

Pansy's eyes widened. "You're a delight. I can tell. I was just a making lunch for all of us. I would love to make you something as well."

"That sounds wonderful. I haven't eaten in a long time," Asta admitted.

"Why not?" Litney asked with concern.

"Gunner was here with his gun. I didn't think it was wise to come out," the bear replied.

"Where were you hiding?" Litney asked as the two of them headed back toward the house.

Asta didn't answer. Instead, she collapsed to the ground. Then Litney heard it: a gunshot.

"No, oh no. Asta," Litney cried, her voice breaking as she sank down next to the furry body. This was Asta. Asta who had done her best to protect her. Asta who loved her. She couldn't—

"Are you all okay?" Gunner yelled, running up to them.

"You shot her!" Litney screamed at him. "How could you shoot her?"

Gunner scratched his head as Talmoon made it into the yard. "I heard Pansy scream," Gunner said. "I saw a bear only two feet away from you. Why wouldn't I have shot it? It's a bear. It could have killed you."

"This bear was their friend," Pansy explained as she knelt down next to Litney. "How bad it is?"

Litney peered at the bear's fur. The blood seemed to be coming from Asta's shoulder. "I don't know. I can't tell."

Talmoon joined them beside the bear. "He hit her in the shoulder. I don't think he hit her heart, but there's a lot of blood." He looked at his wife. "Tell us what we can do."

"Litney," Pansy said as she stood up, her voice sounding like a general's. "I need you to push on the wound with your hand. We have to stop the blood. Talmoon, go to the shed and gather the herbs for a poultice. Dokken, in the closet down the hall there are sheets. Tear them into strips and bring them out here."

Litney commenced pressing on the bear's shoulder. Talmoon left at a lope for the shed, and Dokken dashed inside the house.

"What can I do?" Gunner asked, his eyes wild. "I thought I was protecting you all, but man, I just messed it up again."

Pansy touched his arm. "I screamed and you did what you thought needed to be done to save us. Can you help Litney press on the wound? The two of you pushing on it will help slow the blood flow down even more."

Gunner knelt beside Litney. She didn't move to make room for him to help her. "Look, kid, I'm sorry."

"You shot her," Litney accused, her eyes shimmering with tears.

"I thought you were in trouble," Gunner explained, his silver hair shining in the sun. "I'm sorry. I feel awful."

"You should. Because not only did you shoot her, you pushed us down that well. Twice!" Litney blurted out. "You're a bully. And all for what? Because you were jealous of your brother?"

"Look, I'm not proud of what I've done. Believe me. But let me help now. You aren't big enough. See? Blood's still seeping out. Please let me help."

Litney looked down at her hands. She couldn't stop the flow of red. She moved to make some room and let Gunner's large hands cover her own.

Pansy must have decided the two of them could be left alone, because she dashed inside, saying over her shoulder, "I'll start boiling some water."

Before long, Talmoon returned with a handful of leaves and cheesecloth. He took them inside, and Litney could hear him ask Pansy where to put them. "On the table," she replied. "Pack the herbs between two pieces of cheesecloth."

Litney bent down and whispered into the bear's ear, "Asta, can you hear me?"

The bear moaned.

"We're going to save you, okay?"

No response.

Litney looked down at Gunner's hands which covered her own; no red seemed to be coming up between his fingers. Maybe they were getting the blood slowed. But there was still a lot of blood in Asta's fur and some had even started to pool on the dirt beneath her. "Asta?" she whispered again.

Still no response. "Is she going to be all right?" she asked, turning her frightened eyes to Gunner. She didn't want to talk to him necessarily, but she needed someone, anyone, to tell her it was going to be okay.

"If anyone can fix your friend, it's Pansy."

"I hope so. Asta, you're going to be okay. I promise. You have to be okay," Litney begged.

Talmoon came out of the house, carrying what looked like a cookie sheet. It had white guazy pieces on it filled with leafy things. Pansy followed him with a small pot in one hand and a bottle in her other. "I have a bigger pot of water on to boil, but we'll start with this one." She knelt down beside Litney and asked, "How is the blood flow?"

"I think we've stopped it for the moment."

"Good. But now you're going to have to let go," Pansy said.

"But if we let go, the blood will start again," Litney argued.

"Yes, but we need to get the bullet out of her. Otherwise it will get infected and kill her much more slowly and painfully than bleeding to death."

Litney looked to Talmoon and Gunner, hoping one of them would disagree with Pansy. Gunner said, "It has to be done. Ready? Let's lift up slowly now." She felt the weight of Gunner's hands on her own lessen, but she couldn't bring herself to peel her own off of Asta's wound.

"Litney," Talmoon said quietly from above. "You have to let go."

"I love her," Litney explained. "She's like a second mother. I love her."

"We know," Pansy said, touching her shoulder, "but we have to do this to save her. Come on, pull your hands away. That's it." As soon as the wound was exposed, Pansy pulled a pair of needle-nosed pliers out of her apron pocket and dipped them in the boiling water. Then she warned the bear, "Asta, if you can hear me, this is going to hurt, but we have to do it, okay?" The bear didn't respond. Pansy looked at her husband. "Talmoon, I need you to hold her muzzle. She might be in too much pain to know we are trying to help her. Gunner, can you get her paws?"

The men moved into position. Pansy poured the contents of the bottle onto the wound. Litney saw a label that told her it was whisky. As soon as the liquid hit the bear's wound, her body arched and a roar split the air. "Hold her!" Pansy shouted, digging into the wound with the long thin pliers.

Litney began to cry, horrified as she watched the scene unfolding before her. Talmoon shoved Asta's face to the ground as hard as he could while Gunner laid on the bear's powerful arms to keep them from swiping at any of them. Meanwhile, Pansy continued to work the pliers into the hole. "I can't get it!" she yelled. "It's too deep."

By this time, blood was pulsing out of Asta, making a hard job almost impossible. What if they couldn't get the bullet out? What if Asta died a slow and painful death? Or what if she died right then from blood loss?

Dokken ran out the door with a bundle of torn sheets in his arms. "What should I do—oh my gosh!" he exclaimed when he saw the scene before him. He and Litney locked eyes. "They can't get the bullet," Litney cried. "If they can't get the bullet—"

Dokken's jaw clenched as he saw the men struggling to keep the bear from attacking them and Pansy. "There has to be some way. I know. The bracelet! Litney, you can use the bracelet to coax the bullet out."

Hoping the bracelet would obey her and not put up a fight, Litney waded into the mayhem. "Pansy, get out of the way. I can do this."

"Litney," Pansy said, panting, "this is dangerous. I can get it. I think I can get it."

"No, really. Believe me. I can do this," Litney coaxed. "Please, hurry and move."

Pansy backed out of the way, and Litney slipped into her place next to Asta's back. She pointed the bracelet at the bear's wound. "Come out," she whispered. "Come here. I need you to come here."

"What in the world are you doing?" Gunner demanded. "You can't get a bullet out by asking it to come out. Are you insane?"

Litney ignored him. "Come on. Come out."

"I can see it!" Talmoon yelled since his face was right by the bear's wound. "Keep doing whatever it is you are doing. It's working."

"Come on, come out, come on, come out," Litney chanted.

"What's she doing?" Gunner asked Dokken who was standing above him.

Dokken explained. "Her bracelet. It's magic."

Gunner's eyes narrowed. "Is that what made my bottom burn?"

Dokken gave a slight smile. "Yep."

"It's out," Talmoon said as the bullet tumbled out into the bloody fur. "See it?"

Litney wasn't done yet. She pulled out the yellow purse and took a handful of flowers from it, pushing them into the wound. It had worked for Roonan, and so she was sure this would help save Asta. As she pressed the blossoms, she murmured, "Stop the blood and take away her pain. Please, stop the blood and take away her pain."

Asta's body began to relax. Talmoon didn't have to hold her muzzle so tightly, and Gunner didn't have to hold her paws so hard.

"The poultice," Pansy said, springing back into action. "Let's get it on there. Then, Dokken, hand me some sheets. We need to get this blood stopped again."

Litney withdrew her hands as Pansy slipped the poultice on the wound over the flowers. But as she backed away to let the men apply pressure to the the bear's shoulder, she noticed Asta wasn't moving much. She thought this was a good thing—with the bracelet's help, she had calmed the bear down. And those flowers had saved Roonan—they had to do the same for Asta.

"She's lost a lot of blood," Pansy whispered to Talmoon.

"Too much?"

"I can hear you, you know," Litney said. "She's going to be okay now. We got the bullet out, you're getting the blood slowed down again, those flowers saved Roonan, and look, she's calm now."

Talmoon looked at Litney. "Honey, she's lost a lot of blood."

"I know, but we're stopping it now. It's okay, right?"

Pansy said, "Her breathing. It's gone all choppy. Litney, maybe you'd better go inside. Dokken, why don't you take Litney inside?"

"No!" Litney shouted, jerking her arm away from Dokken when he tried to lead her away. "I won't leave her. Didn't you hear? I love her. She's like a mother to me. I have to stay here."

Gunner, who no longer needed to hold the bear's paws, stood. "Litney, come on. Let's go inside." When he reached out to take her elbow like Dokken, she shoved at his stomach.

"Don't touch me!" she yelled.

"Gunner," Talmoon said with a nod.

"Come on, Litney. We're going inside." This time it was not an invitation. He grabbed her around the waist, threw her over his shoulder, and carried her into the kitchen.

She kicked at him and even tried biting at his back, but he did not put her down until they were inside. Then he released her, blocking her attempts to get back out the door. "I have to get back out there. I have to be with her! I can get those flowers to work," she cried, pummeling his chest with her fists. "Don't you dare try to stop me. You. This is all your fault. All of this."

"Look, kid, I'm sorry. I didn't know. I really didn't know."

Litney tried several more times to push her way through the door, but there was no way she was going to get past Gunner. She sank to the floor, all the way to the floor, so that even her head was resting on the wooden boards. She was crying so hard that her tears made her body convulse. Without knowing it, her weeping was making her worm her way across the floor.

It wasn't until her cheek landed in the gooey glob of leftover tea from the bottom of the shattered teapot that her tears started to relent. "Gross," she moaned, wiping at her face and seeing a mixture of both sludge and blood. She thought the blood was leftover from Asta, but Gunner said, "You've cut your cheek pretty badly on one of the shards. Here, let's get you cleaned up." There was a pause as he bent over her, and then Gunner exclaimed, "Holy Moses!"

"What?" Litney asked, brushing at her cheek. "I know it's gross. I'll wash it off. I was worried about more important things."

"No. Your cut. It's gone. I saw it. It was there, but now it's gone. Completely gone."

"How can that be?" Litney asked, looking at the bracelet, thinking that must be the answer. But the bracelet's stone was cool and dark.

"It's the sludge," Gunner said, wiping a finger across her cheek. "It's this sludge. It made your wound disappear. And why not? It was in the teapot for days. It probably grew extra potent.

"We could—" Litney began.

"—use this on Asta," Gunner finished. "Hurry, let's scrape up as much as we can."

The two of them clawed at the floor, scooping up the green sludge. Then they ran outside.

"We can save her," Gunner yelled.

"I think it's too late," Pansy whispered, her hair wild and her beautiful eyes full of tears. "She's just about gone. I'm so sorry, Litney."

"No, Gunner's right. We can save her. Please get that stuff off her wound and then let us in," Litney begged, skidding to her knees when Pansy had pulled the makeshift bandages and flowers off. Litney began slopping the green stuff onto Asta's wound. "Here," she said to Gunner when she had applied all of hers. "Your turn."

She moved aside and Gunner slipped in beside the bear, piling what was in his hands onto the wound. Then, for good measure, Litney pointed the bracelet at the bear's shoulder. "The flowers must not have any power in this world, so please help this work," she whispered. "Please let this stuff save her."

A gentle light shone from the bracelet onto the bear. Litney closed her eyes, partly because she was too afraid to see if this was going to help, but also because she knew she needed to think good thoughts. Powerful thoughts to make this work.

"Litney, she's opening her eyes!" Dokken said, shaking her shoulder. "Look!"

Litney bent her head so it was right next to the bear's. Asta whispered, "What happened?"

In the awkward silence, Gunner admitted, "I shot you. I thought you were attacking Pansy. I heard her scream. I'm sorry."

"How bad is it?"

"It was pretty bad, but I think," Litney paused and sought Pansy's face. The woman smiled and nodded, so Litney continued, "I think you are going to be okay."

Current, who had been doing his mad circling this entire time, finally came to sit on the other side of Asta. "That was too close," the dog declared.

"I thought you wanted me gone," Asta said slowly, wheezily.

"Not anymore. Why else would I have continued to come and visit you while you were hiding? We talked about so many things."

"I thought you were just checking up on me," Asta said, "making sure I wasn't harming anything in the barn."

Current got a look on his face that could only be described as a caught-with-your-hand-in-the-cookie-jar smile. "Well, that, too. But I liked talking to you. I, uh, would like to talk to you more. I hope you stick around." Then Current backed away, saying, "That is, if Talmoon and Pansy will let you."

"A bear on the property?" Talmoon mused. "I don't know."

"Don't you want to go back to your own world?" Litney asked the bear, wondering what in the world was going on. It seemed like the dog had a thing for Asta. Did that happen in the animal world?

"I don't know if I want to go back to my world," Asta replied, sighing. Her eyes closed again.

Pansy broke in, "She can certainly stay if she wants to, but she can decide that later. Right now, we better let her rest so she can heal."

Talmoon bent over to examine Asta's wound. "She won't have much healing to do. That bracelet and the sludge did a doozy of a good job." He turned his attention to Litney. "That's some bracelet."

"Yes, it is," Litney replied, then she explained, "it gets passed down to all the girls in my family."

"A magic heirloom," Pansy said with a laugh.

When Litney saw Gunner looking at her wrist, she covered her bracelet and said, "Don't you dare."

Gunner smiled and shook his head. "I wouldn't dream of it. No. I have other things I need to do now. But I am sorry. About everything. Could I, uh, could I come and visit you all sometimes?"

Since Talmoon seemed too shocked to answer, it was left to his wife to say happily, "Yes. Yes. Yes."

Gunner gave a half salute and walked off through the wetlands.

"Can you believe it?" Pansy asked no one in particular.

"Nope," Litney and Dokken both said at the same time.

Talmoon, shook his head then he muttered, "Excuse me. I need to go to my barn."

Pansy, Litney and Dokken watched Talmoon go, each of them knowing he probably needed some time alone after everything that had happened to him.

"We should probably get going as well," Litney said and Dokken nodded hard. "Our parents are probably wondering where we are. It was wonderful to meet you all. Glad you're safe and sound, and thanks for helping with Asta. Oh, will you be able to take care of her? Maybe I should stay."

"No, you get on home," Pansy said, locking elbows with the two of them, the same way she had when they had first met her. "I'll take good care of her. And it appears so will Current."

The three of them looked back at the dog who was lying beside the bear's head. He wasn't moving, his body wasn't humming, he was simply being there for her.

"Are you going to leave her there?" Dokken asked, gazing up at the sky which was darkening over to the west.

"No, in a bit, I'll go get Talmoon and have him put a blanket under her. Then he can drag her—gently, of course—to the barn. That should be a nice restful place for her to heal."

They walked a bit more and came to the edge of the farm. "Pansy, can we come back?" Litney asked. "To visit Asta?"

"Of course you can come back to visit Asta, but," Pansy said, giving each of them a kiss on the cheek. "I hope you can come back to visit us as well. Maybe Talmoon could show you how to throw pots."

"Throw pots?" Dokken asked, suddenly confused. "You mean, like, break them?"

"No, silly," Pansy laughed her musical laugh. "I mean create them. That's what it's called. Throwing."

"Oh," Dokken said, his eyes lighting up. "That'd be great. I've always wanted to try that. Growing up in the city, I never got to play in the mud. I was always jealous when I read about kids who could do that."

"Yes, please come back so you can play in the mud." Pansy's face shone with the power of her smile, but then it sobered as she said, "You know, a simple thank you doesn't quite do it. I still don't know what they did to him, but I know it was horrible. Thank you for saving us. For saving him."

"It was our pleasure," Litney said, and then she laughed. "Well, maybe not our pleasure, but we were glad to do it."

Pansy hugged each of them, then waved as Litney and Dokken headed back through the wetlands.

⁂ 17 ⁂

"LIKE THIS?" DOKKEN ASKED Talmoon, who stood behind him.

"Yes. That's wonderful," Talmoon answered as he watched Dokken shaping the clay on the pottery wheel that spun between his legs. "You're a natural."

"I don't believe the same thing can be said for me," Litney sighed as the bowl she was working on collapsed in on itself for the eighth time. "I can't get this clay centered."

"Let me show you again," Talmoon said, squatting beside her. His hands went to the clay and it was as if the clay jumped up, eager to do the man's bidding. The clay zoomed up and down, up and down, and then as soon as Talmoon started pressing his thumbs into the middle of the column of clay, a bowl appeared so quickly, so surely, it was almost as if it was magic. "The trick is to breathe and lean into it. Invite the clay to form itself. Don't tell it what to do."

"I hate it when my parents tell me what to do," Litney admitted.

"The clay feels the same way," Talmoon said, releasing his hands from the bowl he had made as gently as if he were releasing a bowl of the finest crystal. The bowl might have been an infected-gray color, but it was still one of the most beautiful things Litney had ever seen. She wasn't sure why. Maybe because it was balanced and elegant and curvy in all the right places.

"Now it's your turn," Talmoon invited, smushing the beautiful bowl until it was a dull lump of clay once again.

"How can you do that?" Litney cried. "It was so beautiful, and you just destroyed it."

Talmoon shrugged and pointed at the raspberry bushes to their right that were more brown than green now. "You have to learn to let go of things, even if they are beautiful."

Dokken, with a smart smile, asked, "Have you been able to do that with the teapot yet? Let it go?"

Talmoon laughed. "Pansy's probably doing a better job at that than I am, but I don't have a choice now, do I?"

"Can I ask you something?"

"Sure, Litney," Talmoon said.

"Gunner said something that made me think you got the teapot from some Native Americans. Is that true?"

Talmoon went over to a sink and rinsed the clay from his hands. "Yes. I was friends with their chief, and one day, he gave me a bundle of deer skins, saying he wanted to thank me for helping out his people. I brought them three cows that winter, which was probably the longest and coldest one I have ever experienced. When I unwrapped the bundle, inside was that teapot. He gave me this odd smile and told me to use it wisely. I didn't know what he meant until about ten years later. I had been having tea from it every morning, but I never thought anything about it until Gunner stopped by one night. I saw how old he looked, he saw how young I looked, and he demanded to know what was going on. I told him I didn't know. I couldn't imagine how it was happening. It wasn't long after that that Pansy came out here and found me. One day when I poured myself some tea, she stared at my face. She said, 'You're glowing.' I told her to quit horsing around, but she said, 'I mean it. You're glowing.' It took us awhile, but we finally figured out it was the teapot." As he wiped his hands thoughtfully on a towel, he said quietly, "When I fell in love with Pansy, I didn't realize Gunner had fallen in love with her as well. We had a huge fight one night, and then he left and didn't return. But by that point, we had started sharing the tea with him; we had just never told him how it was made. To keep him quiet about it, I sent him some tea once a year. The rest, as they say, is history."

"We thought the same thing about Litney," Dokken said. "That she glowed after she had had some tea. I wonder how it worked," he mused.

"Who knows?" Talmoon said.

"Do you know how Gunner met up with the Gadlanders?" Litney asked.

"Nope. We haven't talked much about that."

"But you have seen him, right?" Dokken asked. "He said he might come by here sometimes."

"Yep, he was here just last week. We had dinner and for the first time in a long time, neither of us wanted to strangle the other."

"So how old are you exactly?" Dokken asked.

"I quit counting awhile ago. Somewhere between a hundred and two hundred."

"Boy, and I thought fifty sounded old," Litney said, punching Talmoon in the arm. She had given up trying to throw her pot and had washed her hands. But as soon as she hit the big man, she couldn't believe she had done it. She smiled uncertainly at him and twisted the bracelet on her wrist. It hadn't disappeared yet, and while she didn't use it, she was glad to have it. She wondered if it was hers to keep.

He hesitated for a moment, but then his big hand tousled her hair. As if embarrassed by this sudden display, he pulled his hand back and turned to Dokken, and saying in that big booming voice of is, "Wow, Dokken. That's a heckuva bowl. Are you sure you haven't done this before?"

"Nope, but I hope I can do it again," he said with a grin that made his entire freckled face shine.

"I think that can be arranged," Pansy said as she entered the studio carrying a tray filled with steaming mugs. "Hot cocoa, anyone?"

"I'd love some, as long as I don't have to try throwing any more bowls," Litney said with a laugh. "Pottery is pretty, but it is not my thing."

"Oh, you never know," Pansy said as she put down the tray and handed Litney a mug. "I told you I came out here looking for Talmoon so he could teach me. What I didn't tell you was that I frustrated him so much with my ineptitude that he sent me packing." She looked up lovingly at the big man, who seemed embarrassed.

"You're kidding," Litney said with a laugh as she plopped three marshmallows into the cocoa. "What happened?"

"I walked back through the wetlands, crying. I remember yelling at my hands. I told them all I wanted to do was to throw pots, so why weren't they cooperating?"

"And how did your hands answer?" Dokken asked with a smirk as he washed his own hands off in the sink.

"They didn't answer me, Mr. Smarty Pants," she said with that arched eyebrow of hers. "My ankle did."

"Your ankle answered you?" Litney asked.

"My ankle told me to go back."

"And how did it do that?" Dokken asked, trying, not very successfully, to keep a straight face.

"By stepping in a hole and getting sprained. I had to hobble back here, my face all streaked from dirt and tears. Talmoon took one look at me, laughed, then scooped me up and carried me into the kitchen to fix my ankle. He proposed an hour later," Pansy said, the lights in her eyes dancing. "And speaking of proposing," she continued, "I think there's another romance blossoming around here."

Because Pansy was looking back and forth between Litney and Dokken, the two of them began to blush. "Uh," Litney started.

"Um," Dokken stuttered.

"Asta and Current," Pansy said, that smile of hers in full bloom. "I'm so glad she decided to stick around. I think it's great."

"Yes, it is," Litney agreed, a little too loudly, going over to the old bookshelf and looking at all the things it housed.

"You bet," Dokken agreed, setting down his mug and doing his best to hide his red face by bending down to tie his shoe that didn't need to be tied.

That's why neither of them saw Pansy wink at Talmoon as she repeated, "Yep, I think the budding romance is great. Just great."

Acknowledgments

I doubt there would have been a Talmoon if I hadn't experienced the breathtaking art and generous hospitality of the potters Richard Bresnahan and Sam Johnson—thank you for welcoming me into your studios and for creating beautiful pieces of pottery that I use every day. In addition, much gratitude to Len Edgerly for his wisdom, Keith Karlson for his sound advice, Trista Morstad for buying copy after copy of *The Bracelet,* Jane Opitz for her grammatical wizardry, as well as Kim Hunter-Perkins, Robin Murray, Anna-Elise Price and Olga Abella for their editorial and motivational gifts. My mother's support—as well as the support of all those I call family—has been amazing, and once again, it was a delight to work with North Star Press. Thanks to my son, Ben, for not wanting to read the book until it was published because he wanted to experience it as a real reader, and to my daughter, Elise, for having the guts to tell me the first version of *The Fountain* wasn't good enough (because you were right). As ever, thanks to Shane for, well, everything.